Down in the dark something had moved. A giant shape was almost directly below them and rising fast.

"There!" Shakespeare cried.

"Paddle!" Nate shouted. But he only stroked twice before the canoe gave a violent lurch and lifted half a foot out of the water. Grabbing the sides, he clung on as the canoe smacked back down with a loud *whomp*, and water splashed in.

The creature promptly disappeared.

"Did you see him?" Shakespeare said, laughing in delight. "Did you see the size of him?"

Nate had seen little beyond the suggestion of great bulk. "We need to get out of here."

"No! It might come back."

"That's what I'm afraid of." Nate peered down, and sure enough, the bulk was rising toward them again. "It's going to hit us!"

Recent books in the Wilderness series:

For a full listing, turn to the back of this book.

WILDERNESS #56:
In Darkest Depths

David Thompson

LEISURE BOOKS NEW YORK CITY

Dedicated to Judy, Shane, Joshua and Kyndra.

A LEISURE BOOK®

June 2008

Published by

Dorchester Publishing Co., Inc.
200 Madison Avenue
New York, NY 10016

ISBN 10: 0-8439-5932-0
ISBN 13: 978-0-8439-5932-1

The name "Leisure Books" and the stylized "L" with design are trademarks of Dorchester Publishing Co., Inc.

Printed in the United States of America.

10 9 8 7 6 5 4 3 2 1

Visit us on the web at www.dorchesterpub.com.

WILDERNESS #56:
In Darkest Depths

David Thompson

LEISURE BOOKS NEW YORK CITY

First Incident

To the bald eagle flying high in the Rocky Mountain sky, the lake was a great blue egg in the center of the lush green nest of the valley floor.

To the girl standing on the lake's western shore, it was a constant source of entertainment and wonderment. She loved to gaze out over its watery expanse and watch the ducks and geese swim and dive for fish. She fished herself, now and then, and this was one of those occasions.

Evelyn King had not yet seen her seventeenth birthday. The daughter of mountain man Nate King and Nate's Shoshone wife, Winona, Evelyn had more of her father in her than her mother. Sparkling green eyes and lustrous black hair testified to her blossoming beauty, of which she was wholly unconscious. She still thought of herself as a girl, not a woman. She still liked to take her father's fishing pole and spend an idle hour fishing and thinking.

On this particular bright sunny day, Evelyn was perched on a small boulder, humming to herself as she watched the bald eagle soar with outstretched pinions. She wore a beige dress she had sewn herself, patterning it after the latest St. Louis fashion.

Evelyn was watching the eagle, but she was thinking of Degamawaku. She thought of him a lot. He and his family were Nansusequa, a tribe from east of the Mississippi River. Forced to flee when whites wiped out their village, the family had settled in King Valley, as it was called, with her father's consent. She had been spending a lot of time in Dega's company of late. He was her age and fun to be with and strikingly handsome.

As Evelyn sat humming and wondering about the intent looks Dega gave her from time to time, she heard the tread of approaching footsteps. Thinking he was coming to pay her another visit, she swiveled and smiled her warmest smile, only to have it die stillborn and be replaced by a frown. "Oh. It is only you."

The white-haired man in buckskins, a Hawken rifle cradled in the crook of his left elbow, blinked eyes the same color as the lake and puffed out his full cheeks. "I dare say, that was as warm a greeting as I have ever received. How now, girl? Dost thou jeer and flout me in the teeth?" he said.

"Hello, Uncle Shakespeare," Evelyn said. "I am glad to see you."

"So you claim," Shakespeare McNair responded. "But I was not born yesterday. Nor ten thousand yesterdays ago." Again he quoted his namesake, "Let the candied tongue lick absurd pomp."

Evelyn grinned and asked, "What does that mean, exactly? Or is my pa right in saying that when you quote the Bard, you have no notion of what the Bard is saying?"

A pink tinge of indignation spread from Shakespeare's neck to his brow. He was sensitive about his namesake. "Horatio said that?" he sputtered. "Why, he hath more hair than wit and more faults than hair."

Laughing, Evelyn lowered the pole to her lap. "I love it when you talk like that. You are just like an old billy goat."

Shakespeare's indignation increased. "And to think, I used to bounce you on my knee and make funny faces so you would grin and giggle."

Evelyn adored McNair. He was not really her uncle. He was her father's best friend and mentor, and as much a part of their family as any blood relation. More so, since he had many times shown his love for them by risking life and limb in their defense. "What brings you out and about on this fine summer morning?"

McNair hunkered next to the boulder. In addition to his rifle, he was armed with a brace of pistols and a bone-handled hunting knife. An ammo pouch, powder-horn, and a possibles bag were slanted crosswise over his chest. "That wretch I share my cabin with kicked me out. She was cleaning and said I was underfoot."

"Oh, Uncle Shakespeare," Evelyn said. "That's no way to talk about the woman you love."

"Says who?" McNair rejoined. "A pox on all females! As for my wife, we cannot call her winds and waters sighs and tears. They are greater storms and tempests than almanacs can report." Teasing women was one of his favorite pastimes.

"You know," Evelyn said. "I like how you always quote from that big book you have on the real Shakespeare. But half the time I have no idea what you are saying."

"My apologies, child. I just said my wife is a moody wench."

"Blue Water Woman is one of the sweetest people I know," Evelyn remarked. "She adores you and you adore her, and don't pretend you don't."

"Adore!" Shakespeare snorted. "I will praise an eel with the same praise as I do that—" He abruptly stopped.

The pole had given a jerk. Evelyn gripped it firmly and saw the line go taut. "I have a bite!" she said in delight. She hoped it was a big one. She and her brother, Zach, had an ongoing contest to see who could catch the biggest fish, and a couple of months ago he had landed one that weighed close to five pounds.

Shakespeare shot to his feet. His entire life he had been an avid fisherman, as much for the sport as the eating. "Careful now," he cautioned. "Let it have some line if it wants it."

"I know."

"The trick is to tire it out. Then you can bring it in nice and easy," Shakespeare went on.

"I know that, too," Evelyn said. "My pa taught me all about how to fish."

"I am only trying to help. Do I look like a cudgel or a hovel-post, a staff or a prop?"

"What?" Evelyn said, and nearly lost the pole when it tried to leap out of her hands. Holding fast, she stood and braced her legs. "Did you see that?" she exclaimed in amazement.

"You have caught a whale," Shakespeare said.

Evelyn strained to hold on to the pole. "It must be huge! Wait until Zach sees what I've caught."

"There are two things in life we should never do, child," Shakespeare said. "One is to put the horse before the cart, and the other is to put the fish before the frying pan."

The line went slack, but Evelyn was sure the fish was still on the hook. "What is he up to?"

"He?" Shakespeare repeated. "How do you know it is not a she? If it is contrary, it must be female."

"To hear you talk, a body would think you do not cuddle with your wife three times a week."

Shakespeare imitated a riled chipmunk. "Why, Evelyn King! Wait until I tell your mother what you just said. She will brand you a wanton."

"For talking about cuddling?" Evelyn was about to tell him she once overheard Blue Water Woman mention to her mother how frisky he was, but the line went taut, and the end of the pole curled toward the water. It was all she could do to hold on. "Dear Lord."

"A by-God whopper, girl!" Shakespeare exclaimed. "Whatever you do, don't lose him."

"Him? I thought you just told me it has to be female—" Evelyn got no further. The pole jumped toward the lake, and she went with it, digging in her heels to keep from falling on her face. "Help me!"

In a bound Shakespeare reached her side. He grabbed the pole with his free hand and was amazed when it bent even more.

"What do we do?" Evelyn asked.

Before Shakespeare could answer, the line broke with a loud *snap*. He lunged but missed, and the line disappeared into the water, leaving tiny swirls in its wake.

"Drat," Evelyn said in disgust. "It got away."

"Fish do that," Shakespeare philosophized. Secretly, though, he could not help but be astounded.

"You don't suppose . . . ?" Evelyn let her question trail off.

"No, I don't."

They looked at each other and then at the lake, and Evelyn said softly, as if afraid to be heard, "You're probably right. Why would it go after a measly worm? It was a fish, nothing more."

"It was a fish," Shakespeare said.

But neither believed it.

Second Incident

To most whites, Blue Water Woman was a Flathead. Her people, however, called themselves the Salish. They lived well to the north of King Valley in a region that boasted the largest body of fresh water between the Mississippi River and the Pacific Ocean. King Lake was not nearly as big as Flathead Lake, as that other lake was known, but to her it was the jewel in their new home.

As a girl, Blue Water Woman had whiled away many an idle hour at Flathead Lake. She and her friends frolicked in the shallows and swam every chance they got. She often went for long swims away from shore, despite repeated warnings from her parents and others.

Not long ago, when Shakespeare told her about Nate King's plan to move all of them from the foothills to a valley deep in the mountains, she nearly said she was against the idea. Then her husband mentioned that the valley boasted a lake and they would live along its shore. In a heartbeat she changed her mind. "If you want to do it, we will."

"Ha, ha! Are you honest?" Shakespeare had asked.

"What do you mean?" Blue Water Woman suspected he was quoting old William S, as Shakespeare called his namesake.

"That if you be honest and fair, your honesty should admit no discourse to your beauty."

"I am always honest and fair with you. If you want to move, then I want to move. You are my husband and my heart, and I would not live without you."

Blue Water Woman smiled at the memory. Shakespeare had been touched by her declaration of love, and for a few days had treated her with extra tenderness. He had even forgotten to be grumpy, which, given his usual disposition, was a miracle in and of itself. He was not truly happy unless he was complaining about something or other.

Chuckling, Blue Water Woman bent to the task at hand. She was out behind their cabin on the south shore of the lake, squatting at the water's edge, wringing out towels and a blanket. It was laundry day, which for her meant carrying whatever needed washing to the lake and giving it a good dunking.

The breeze off the lake was cool, although the day was hot. She raised her head and turned her face so the breeze caught her full-on. A sense of peace and contentment came over her and she closed her eyes.

Blue Water Woman was happy with her life. She had a husband who adored her, a man she loved with all her being, a comfortable cabin in which to live, horses and chickens and even several piglets. She was within short walking distance of her dearest friend, Winona King. Her only other neighbors were Winona's son, Zach, and Zach's wife, Lou, who had a cabin on the north shore, and the Nansuseqa family to the east of the lake.

A loud splash ended her reverie. She opened her

eyes and spied concentric circles spreading across the surface of the lake a stone's throw out. She assumed that a fish had surfaced and gone back under, and she started to bend to the towels.

Suddenly Blue Water Woman froze.

Something was floating under the water near the concentric circles. She could not quite make out what it was, but it was big, far bigger than any fish she'd ever seen or heard of. She thought it must be a trick of the sunlight, a shadow of some kind, but when she tilted her head, it did not go away. Whatever it was, it was real.

The warnings of her early years returned to fill her with dread. Annoyed at herself for being so silly, she began to rise, but she stopped when she realized the thing was coming toward her.

Blue Water Woman's heart beat faster. She remembered the stories vividly, accounts of creatures that dwelled in Flathead Lake and others. Creatures that lived in the depths and only came to the surface on rare occasions. Creatures, her people believed, that were bad medicine. That should be avoided. Creatures that ate people.

In her early years, Blue Water Woman had thought the stories silly. Tales her mother told to keep her from swimming alone. She had ignored the warnings and done as she pleased.

Then came the day her opinion had changed. She had seen fourteen winters. It had been early spring, and her people were camped close to Flathead Lake. A warrior had shot a deer with an arrow. Wounded, frantic to escape, the buck had plunged into the lake and swam to a small island not far from shore, and the warrior hurried to a canoe to go after it.

Blue Water Woman had not seen what happened

next. She'd heard about it from her father. He, along with dozens of others, had watched the warrior paddle toward the island. The day had been sunny and clear and the water undisturbed, but midway the canoe unexpectedly shook as if caught in a gust of wind. The warrior had gripped the sides and looked about in consternation.

A few of the Salish said they had seen a dark shape rise out of the deep and strike the bottom of the canoe. But others had seen nothing. Some had shouted for the warrior to forget the buck and come back. But the warrior had gone on paddling.

Everyone had witnessed the consequence: something *did* rise up out of the lake, something bigger than the canoe, striking it with terrible violence and lifting the front end clear out of the water. The warrior had tried to hold on, but he was pitched into the lake. They had seen him flail his arms. They'd heard him cry out. Then, in the blink of an eye, he was gone.

Women had screamed. Children had run. Men had rushed to canoes to go to the warrior's aid, but an elder warned them they must not go into the water. The lake creature was angry, the elder had said. They had not offered a sacrifice to it in many moons, and the hunter had paid the price of their folly. That very night they did as they had done in olden times, and a doe was slain and taken out in a canoe and dropped in the water at the spot where the warrior had gone under.

There'd been no more attacks. Winters had gone by. Blue Water Woman had never seen the creature. The memory and the menace had faded from her mind. She grew up, eventually took McNair for her mate, and moved far away.

Then came the move to King Valley.

Now, strange things were beginning to happen. Waves appeared on the lake when there was no wind. The water would roil and churn with no visible cause. They heard loud splashing, but no fish jumped. Nearly all of them glimpsed *something* out in the water, but none of them could say what it was.

Now this.

Blue Water Woman felt genuine fear as the shape glided slowly toward her. Yet at the same time she was elated that she might at long last see it. Conditions were ideal. It was not raining or misty or foggy, as was often the case when the creature made its presence known.

Then, in a twinkling, the thing was gone. It seemed to sink straight down into the depths and vanish.

Blue Water Woman waited breathlessly for it to reappear. Suddenly a hand fell on her shoulder, and she jumped and spun, her hand dropping to the knife she was never without. "Oh!" she exclaimed in her husband's tongue. "It is only you."

Shakespeare McNair grinned. "That is a fine way to greet me. My mistress with a monster is in love," he quoted. Then he saw her eyes. "What is the matter?"

Blue Water Woman threw her arms around him and held him close. She quaked, although she could not say why. "Oh, Carcajou," she said, using the name he was known by of old, her special term of endearment for him.

"I repeat," Shakespeare said, shocked by her reaction. He could count the number of times he had seen his wife like this on one hand and have fingers left over. "What is the matter?"

"I saw it," Blue Water Woman said.

"Saw what?"

"It."

Shakespeare gazed out over the placid lake but saw only a few mallards. "The thing?"

Blue Water Woman shuddered again.

"Did you get a good look? What is it?"

"I could not see much," Blue Water Woman said.

"Yet you are this scared?" Shakespeare had seen his wife stand up to a grizzly without flinching.

"I think it was—" Blue Water Woman caught herself. "No. That is silly. I must be wrong."

"About what?" Shakespeare prompted.

"I think it knew I was here," Blue Water Woman said, almost in a whisper. "I think it was looking at me."

Shakespeare held her and stroked her and glared at the water. He did not like it when the woman he loved was upset. He did not like it at all. "This is a sorry sight," he quoted.

"I am sorry. I am being childish."

"It is not you. It is *that*," Shakespeare said, with a bob of his snow-colored beard at the blue water. "I am losing my patience with that thing."

"There is nothing we can do," Blue Water Woman said.

"One more incident like this, and I will declare war," Shakespeare vowed.

"No, you will not. My people say we are to have nothing to do with the water devils, as you would call them. To anger them is to court death."

"I am too old for fairy tales."

"Carcajou!" Blue Water Woman drew back and regarded him sternly. "I will thank you not to belittle our beliefs. And I want your word that you will not go out after it."

"Your wish is my command, my dear." But Shakespeare's eyes, fixed on the lake, said different.

Third Incident

Louisa King was giddy with delight. The past few mornings she had woken up feeling queasy. It was a sign, she hoped, that at long last her dream would come true. But she did not say anything to her husband. She wanted to be certain.

On this particular day, Zach had gone off at daybreak with Shakespeare McNair to hunt. They were low on meat, and the valley teemed with deer.

Louisa spent the morning and early afternoon puttering about their cabin. She washed the breakfast dishes. She picked up the clothes Zach had left lying about. She picked up the bullets and patches he left on the table. She put away the whetstone he left on the counter. She cleaned up the feathers he left lying on the bedroom floor.

If Lou had told him once, she had told him a hundred times not to fletch arrows in their bedroom. But did Zach listen? No. Everything she said to him went in one ear and bounced out again.

If there was anything in all creation more aggravating than men, Lou had yet to come across it. Zach was living proof. He had a knack for irritating her in a hundred and one small ways.

Yet for all that, Lou loved him as she had never

loved anyone. He was everything to her: her joy, her peace, her very breath. She could no more imagine life without him than she could imagine life without the sun or the moon.

How strange life could be, Lou mused as she strolled from their cabin to the lake and stood idly admiring the blue sheen of its peaceful surface. When she was young, she'd never expected to fall in love, never figured to take a husband, never believed a man could claim her heart. She thought she would somehow be immune to men. So what if women had been falling in love with them since the dawn of time? She was different. She was special. She was unique.

Lou laughed at her folly. Why was it, she wondered, that people denied their own natures? What made them think the passions that governed the rest of the human race did not govern them? Part of it, she supposed, was just plain silliness. It was ridiculous to imagine that with the millions upon millions of people in the world, and the untold millions who had lived before, that anyone, anywhere, ever had a thought that had not been thought or felt a feeling that had not been felt. It had all been done before. Truly, and literally, there was nothing new under the sun.

A commotion in the water intruded on Lou's pondering. A short way out, small wavelets were rippling the surface, seeming to rise out of nowhere and for no reason.

Lou moved to the water's edge for a better look. She was aware of the creature that supposedly lived in the lake. The Kings and the McNairs talked about it often enough. But she had never seen it and would dearly love to.

Opinions varied. Her husband and father-in-law leaned toward the notion that it was a great fish. Blue Water Woman thought it might be something out of Flathead legend. Shakespeare McNair, of late, had taken to calling the thing a monster.

If Lou could see it, she could settle the debate once and for all.

With that in mind, Lou hunkered so there was less chance of the thing seeing her. The wavelets were growing. Whatever was making them, she deduced, was rising toward the surface. She grinned, every nerve taut, excited that *she* would be the one to solve the mystery.

Something appeared deep down, a dark shape that gave no clue to its identity. Lou had been raised in the wild by her father and had hunted all her life, and she was good at judging size at a distance. But in this instance the best she could conclude was that the thing was longer than a horse and as broad as a buffalo. It boggled her that a fish, if that is what it was, could be so huge.

"Keep coming!" Lou whispered excitedly. "I want a peek at your big self."

But the thing stayed where it was. Several small fish leaped out of the water and swam frantically off, as if in fear of being eaten.

Louisa rose a bit higher for a better look.

Without warning, the thing exploded into motion and shot toward her at frightening speed. Frozen in surprise, Lou did not think to run. She told herself that she was perfectly safe, that she was on land and the creature was a water dweller.

But then the water swelled upward with astonishing rapidity, creating a wave that bore down on Lou with the swiftness of an avalanche. A foot the wave rose, then a foot and a half. Belatedly, Lou started to turn, but she was only halfway around when the wave slammed into her legs. She was bowled over and fell onto her side, the breath whooshing from her lungs. For a harrowing instant she was engulfed in a cold, wet cocoon. Without thinking, she gulped for air and sucked in water. It got into her mouth, into her nose. Gasping, blinking her eyes to clear them, she groped frantically about.

Suddenly Lou's arms were seized, and she was swung into the air as if she were weightless. Involuntarily, she cried out, then saw who had seized her. "Oh! Thank goodness!"

Zach had her by the right arm, Shakespeare by the left. Shakespeare was staring at the lake, but her husband only had eyes for her.

Unlike his sister, Evelyn, Zach had slightly more of his mother in him than his father. He was big, like Nate, and broad of shoulder, like Nate, and had green eyes, like Nate, but his black hair and swarthy complexion and facial features were inherited from Winona. He wore buckskins, and was a walking armory.

"Are you all right?"

"I'm fine," Lou said, embarrassed by her lapse and annoyed that she was soaking wet. She shrugged loose of them. "You are back sooner than I expected."

"Forget that," Zach said, and motioned at the water. "What in God's name happened?"

"I saw it," Shakespeare said.

Zach glanced at him. "What?"

"I saw it!" Shakespeare repeated. "For just a second there, before it dived, I saw the thing that lives in the lake."

"I saw it, too," Lou said. "But I can't tell you what I saw."

Zach looked her up and down and then at the lake, and scowled. "I would like to see it," he said, and wagged his rifle. "Up close, so I can kill it."

"I don't know as it meant to harm me," Lou said.

"I don't care," Zach said. "Nothing hurts you and lives."

Louisa tenderly touched his cheek. "My protector. But there is not much we can do. It's too big to catch and it hardly ever comes to the surface for us to shoot it. I say we leave it be."

"If a bear broke into our cabin while we were away, I would not let the bear live because it might come back when we were there," Zach said. "If a mountain lion stalked our horses, I would hunt it down and shoot it before it killed one of them. This is no different."

"No harm was done," Lou stressed. Then she remembered her morning sickness and the time an aunt lost a baby early on when she fell from a wagon. Pressing a hand to her belly, Lou said, "At least, I hope no harm was done."

"What are you—?" Zach began, and gripped her by the shoulders. "Wait! Are you saying what I think you are saying? You are with child?"

"What's that?" Shakespeare said.

Louisa was disappointed that her surprise might have been spoiled. "I can't say for sure yet, but some of the signs are there, yes."

Whooping for joy, Zach swept her into his arms and spun her in a circle. "A son! We might have a son!"

"Or a daughter," Lou said.

"A boy to teach to ride and shoot and hunt!" Zach said happily.

"Or a *daughter*," Lou said again. It bothered her that whenever the subject of having a baby came up, he always assumed it would be male.

Shakespeare put a hand on her arm. "You better let Winona and my wife have a look at you."

"I'm fine," Lou said. "Besides I'm not certain yet. And I would rather not tell anyone until I know for sure."

"We will keep your secret, but it never hurts to be safe," Shakespeare cautioned, and bestowed a grim glance on the water. "Which is why I can't put it off any longer."

"What are you talking about?" Zach asked.

"That thing," Shakespeare said with a nod. "Whatever it is we keep glimpsing and hearing. It could have killed Lou just now."

"You are making more out of it than there was," Lou assured him.

"I am entitled to my opinion," Shakespeare replied. "And in my opinion, this has gone on long enough. We must find out what it is. Better yet, we must prevent it from ever harming us."

"I call that overreacting," Louisa said.

"I call it prudent," Shakespeare countered. "What if you are right and you are with child?"

Louisa laughed. "I'm pretty sure Zach is the father and not the thing in the lake."

"Poke fun if you want," Shakespeare said. "But if you have a child, he or she will want to play near the water or go for a swim. What happens if the creature does to your offspring what it just did to you?"

"I never thought of that," Lou admitted, troubled at the prospect.

"That is why you young folks need me and my white hair around," Shakespeare said. "So you can benefit from my wisdom." He paused. "I have made up my mind. I am going to find out once and for all what that thing is."

Gilding The Goat

"It is the silliest idea I have ever heard."

Shakespeare McNair glared across the supper table at his wife. "I shall unfold equal discourtesy to your best kindness," he quoted indignantly.

"You could go to a lot of effort for nothing," Blue Water Woman said. "The creature in the lake does not come to the surface often."

"Three times in the past month is not what I would call rare," Shakespeare countered.

"My people say that water devils are bad medicine."

"Devils, as in more than one?"

Blue Water Woman dabbed at her lips with a cloth napkin. She had insisted on using napkins ever since the time they'd had supper with a missionary and the missionary's wife, who thought that no meal was complete without them. "They live in many lakes and rivers."

"I recollect hearing stories," Shakespeare said. He seldom used the napkins she always placed by his plate. To him, it was putting on airs. "I always thought they were tall tales."

"I expect better of you," Blue Water Woman said. Her tone warned Shakespeare she was annoyed.

Given that she had a disposition as mild as milk, he sensed he needed to mend fences. "What did I say? Whites tell tall tales all the time."

"There is a difference," Blue Water Woman said in her impeccable English. "When you and Nate have had a few drinks, you love to tell stories. Black-tail bucks you shot become as big as elk. Bears you killed become twice the size they were when you killed them. Fish you caught that were as long as your hand become as long as your arm."

Shakespeare made a sound that resembled a goose being strangled. "You should be hooted at like one of those old tales," he paraphrased.

"I beg your pardon?"

"Swapping yarns is a tradition with us whites. We do it for the chuckles and the laughs."

"My people have a tradition, too. But the stories we tell are tales of the early times. What whites would call legends or myths. To us they have as much meaning as those stories from the Old Testatment you hold in such high regard."

Shakespeare glanced at the shelf where their Bible and his other books were neatly lined up. At one end was his prized copy of the complete works of William Shakespeare. He'd bought it from an emigrant bound for Oregon Country. At the time he'd simply wanted something to read during the winter months when the streams were frozen and the snow was as high as a cabin and trapping was impossible. Little had he known the passion that would seize him. He adored the Bard's works as he adored no other.

Blue Water Woman had gone on, "I will give you an example. One you have already heard." She paused. "The Salish believe the world was created by

Amotken. He made the first people, but they would not heed him and became wicked so he drowned them in a flood."

"Yes, I know the story," Shakespeare said. "It perked up my ears considerably the first time I heard it since it sounds a lot like the story of Noah and the flood."

"My own ears 'perked up,' as you call it, when you read about the giants that roamed the world in those days," Blue Water Woman replied. "The Coeur d'Alenes say that giants once lived in their country. The giants wore bearskins and painted their faces black and went around at night stealing women."

"Darned peculiar coincidence," Shakespeare said.

"To us, those stories are not tall tales. They are not myths. They are real and true and tell how things were back then. We do not tell them for—how did you put it?—laughs and chuckles."

"Ouch," Shakespeare said. "A hit, a very palpable hit," he quoted from *Hamlet*. He chose his next words carefully. "And you are right. There is a difference between the Bible and the tall tales we whites like to tell. I never meant to suggest that Salish stories of water creatures are hot air, and I apologize if I gave you that idea."

Blue Water Woman grinned. "You are sweet when you grovel."

"How now, woman," Shakespeare retorted. "Again you prick me with that rapier you call a tongue."

"What is wrong with calling you sweet?"

"Thou art so leaky that we must leave thee to thy sinking," Shakespeare said. "It is not the *sweet* I object to."

"I am afraid you have lost me," Blue Water Woman said in feigned innocence.

"Shameless tart," Shakespeare grumbled. "Why is it that when a woman says she is sorry she is apologizing, but when a man says he is sorry he is groveling?"

"Women have too much pride to grovel."

Shakespeare sat back. "Let's change the subject."

"Fine," Blue Water Woman said. "We will go back to the thing in the lake and your silly plan to catch it."

"Change the subject again."

"No. We have not settled this one." Blue Water Woman took a sip of her tea. She was deeply worried, but she did not want her worry to show. Knowing him, he would take it the wrong way. "You are not as young as you used to be," she said.

Shakespeare was taken aback. She hardly ever brought up their ages. Yes, he had seen eighty winters, but he was as spry as a man of sixty, and said so.

"Yes, you have wonderful vitality," Blue Water Woman conceded. "If you were going after a bear or a mountain lion, I would not fret."

"Then why make an issue of this water devil?"

"Because we have no idea what it is," Blue Water Woman said. "It could be very dangerous."

Shakespeare snickered. "If it turns out to be a cow I will be safe enough."

"Scoff all you want, but in the old times there lived many animals that have long since died out. Monsters, whites would call them. Some were as big as buffalo and could live both in the water and on land."

"The thing in this lake has never come out of it," Shakespeare felt compelled to mention.

"My point," Blue Water Woman said, "is that we

are dealing with something we know nothing about. It could be a creature left over from the time before there were people."

Shakespeare was about to tell here that was pure nonsense, but he settled for saying, "That is unlikely, don't you think?"

Blue Water Woman did not appear to hear him. "There were beaver the size of horses and horses the size of beaver. There were cats with teeth as long as a bowie knife, and animals with horns on their noses and others with tusks. Birds so big that when they flapped their wings it sounded like thunder."

"I would like to have ridden one of those," Shakespeare said.

"You are scoffing again."

"Over in a place called the British Isles there are folks who believe in tiny people with wings and little men who dress all in green and cache pots of gold at the ends of rainbows," Shakespeare said. "I scoff at that, too."

Blue Water Woman puckered her mouth in disapproval. "You are not taking this seriously."

"On the contrary," Shakespeare said. "I always listen to what you have to say. But my mind is made up. I want to know what is in the lake, and by God, I will find out."

"Even if it kills you?"

Shakespeare picked up his fork and stabbed a string bean. He wagged it at her, saying, "Is that what this is about?"

"In a word, yes," Blue Water Woman admitted.

"I thought so." Shakespeare stabbed another string bean, then a third. He wagged them at her, too. "Dost thou jeer and flout me in the teeth?"

"I love you."

"Then give me more credit. Yes, I am getting on in years, but I still have all my faculties. I can hike five miles without getting winded, I can ride all day without being saddle-sore, and I do my husbandly duty by you three nights a week."

"I have always liked that part," Blue Water Woman said.

"The duty?"

"How much you enjoy lying with me. Some women say their husbands do not do it nearly as often as you do."

"The night I stop is the day you can plant me," Shakespeare said. "But we have strayed off the trail. I resent the slur that I am old and feeble. I have just as much vim and vinegar as Zach, and he is a lot younger."

"Nate, perhaps," Blue Water Woman said. "But Louisa told me that Zach cannot keep his hands off her. They lay together almost every night."

"The boy is a satyr!" Shakespeare declared. "And what is she doing telling you that? Don't you females keep secrets?"

"No."

About to take a bite of the string beans, Shakespeare paused. "Wait. You haven't told anyone about our bed time, have you?"

"What little there is to tell."

Shakespeare burst into laughter. He laughed so hard he nearly stabbed himself with the fork. When at last he could catch his breath, he beamed at her and said, "That was your finest ever."

"Thank you."

"But let's get this settled once and for all. If I were thirty you would not object to me going after this thing. Heck, if I were fifty you wouldn't squawk."

"Have you looked in a mirror lately? You are neither thirty nor fifty. Nor even sixty."

"White hairs do not a simpleton make, wench. I will thank you to treat me with a little more respect."

Blue Water Woman sighed. Setting down her cup, she rose and came around the table. "I only brought this up because I care." Bending, she embraced him, resting her cheek on his shoulder. "Were I to lose you, my life would be empty."

Shakespeare fidgeted in his chair. "How do you expect me to stay angry with you?"

Blue Water Woman kissed him on the cheek. "I don't."

"Damn your feminine wiles."

"I love you, too."

They kissed again, longer and passionately. When Blue Water Woman pulled away, Shakespeare pushed back his chair and stood.

"I need some air."

"I am sorry I care so much, Carcajou."

"It is my soul that calls upon my name," Shakespeare softly quoted. "How silver-sweet sound lovers' tongues by night, like softest music to attending ears." He smiled and went out, remembering to take his rifle from beside the door. The cool evening air was a welcome relief from the flush of ardor. Overhead, stars had blossomed.

Shakespeare walked to the lake and gazed out over the dark waters. He thought of the thing in the depths, and more of the lines he had read countless times tripped from his troubled lips. "There is special providence in the fall of a sparrow. If it be now, 'tis not to come. If it be not to come, it will be now. If it be not now, yet it will come. The readiness is all."

He stopped, and scowled. "There's the rub. I am not ready. I would savor her until the end of time if I could."

The crunch of a step brought Shakespeare around with his Hawken rising. The tall, broad-shouldered figure strolling toward him showed white teeth in a warm smile.

"I thought I saw you out here," Nate King said.

"Horatio!" Shakespeare delightedly exclaimed, using his pet name for the man he loved as a son. He clapped Nate on the arm. "You are a balm to these tired eyes."

"I just got back from Bent's Fort," Nate related. "I brought the sugar and flour the women wanted and enough powder to last us all for the next year."

"You just got back, you say?" Shakespeare asked. It was a ten-day ride to the trading post and another ten days to return. "How is it you are over here talking to me instead of treating that adorable wife of yours to your company?"

"Winona just told me that you plan to try and catch the creature in the lake."

"Oh, hell," Shakespeare said.

"What is the matter?"

"I am not a dunce. My wife has been talking to your wife and now she sends you to do their handiwork." Shakespeare kicked a stone, and it rolled into the water. "Females! They cut off our heads with a gilded axe and smile as they deliver the killing stroke."

"Was that the Bard?"

"Somewhat," Shakespeare said. "But you can turn around and go right back to your cabin. I want to do it and I will do it, and I don't care who thinks I shouldn't."

Nate grinned. "Stamp your foot a few times and you will remind me of Zach when he was five years old."

"Fah!" Shakespeare rejoined.

"Simmer down."

"I will not. At my age a little simmering is good for the blood."

"It is true what they say, then. The older we get, the younger we act."

"What sock did you pull that one out of? It is mine to do, do you hear me? I will pit brain and sinew against the water devil, and may the real devil take the hindmost."

"Be sure you are right, and then go ahead," Nate said. "That motto worked for Davy Crockett, and it will work for us."

"Us, Horatio?"

"That is why I came over," Nate said. "Remember the grizzly that lived in the valley when we first came here? We tried to live in peace with it, but it chased my son over a cliff and tried to make a meal of my family and me. I had no choice but to kill it." Nate turned toward the lake. "We need to know what is out there and whether it is a danger to our families."

"Then you are not here to talk me out of going after it?"

"On the contrary. I am here to tell you I am with you. We will see this through together."

Shakespeare McNair chortled. "This is the reason you are the manly apple of my eye. To battle, then, Horatio! Unleash the dogs of war!"

Bats in The Belfry

It was not quite ten o'clock the next morning when loud banging and scraping noises drew Blue Water Woman out of her cabin to stare in bewilderment at the roof. Planks left over from the chicken coop were unevenly stacked at one end. In the center, hammering away, was her husband. Their ladder was propped against the side of the cabin, and Nate King was just coming down it.

"Good morning," he greeted her.

"Good morning to you," Blue Water Woman responded, and then focused on the man she had married. "Carcajou?"

Shakespeare went on hammering.

"Do not pretend you cannot hear me," Blue Water Woman said.

With an exaggerated sigh, Shakespeare lowered his hammer and shifted on his knees. "What is it, woman? Can't you see we men are busy at important work?"

"You did not tell me Nate was here."

"Do you expect me to mention every trifle? Should I tell you when I heed Nature's call? Or pick my teeth?"

"Someone got up on the wrong side of the bed this morning, and it was not me."

"Me either," Shakespeare said, selecting a nail. "If my disposition were any sunnier, you could not stand to look at me except on cloudy days."

"What are you doing to my roof?"

Shakespeare reacted as if she had slapped him. "*Your* roof? We both live under it. Which makes it mine as much as yours and entitles me to make improvements if I so desire."

Blue Water Woman put her hands on her hips. "How do you improve a roof that has nothing wrong with it?"

Nate was filling his arms with planks. He looked up at McNair. "You didn't tell her what we are going to do?"

"Stay out of this, Horatio."

"I took it for granted you would," Nate said. To Blue Water Woman he said, "It was his idea. A darned good one, too."

"Perhaps you will share his brilliance with me since he saw fit not to," Blue Water Woman prompted.

"We figure that we need to get a good look at the thing in the lake so we will have a better idea of how to deal with it," Nate explained. "And the higher we are, the more of the lake we can see."

"What does that have to do with my roof?"

Shakespeare slid to the edge and balanced on his hands and knees. "We are building a steeple."

"A what?"

"Do you remember that time we went back East? All the churches we saw with bell towers on top? Those are called steeples."

"You are turning our cabin into a church?"

Shakespeare did his strangled goose impression. "Honestly, woman. The silly notions you come up with. Have I taken out our table and chairs and replaced them with pews? Have I torn down the fireplace and put in an altar?"

"Do not give yourself ideas."

"All I am building is a steeple. Then Nate and I will take turns keeping watch through his spyglass. Our big handicap has been that we can't see much of the lake from the ground, but the steeple will remedy that."

"You couldn't climb a tree?"

Shakespeare made a sweeping motion with his arm. "Show me a single tree anywhere near the water and we will use it instead."

Blue Water Woman couldn't. To the west and north the woods only came to within a hundred yards of the water. To the south grew grass. To the east the forest was slightly closer, but the closest trees were short and thin.

"I thought not," Shakespeare said triumphantly. "Now will you go pester a chipmunk and leave us be?"

"Not so fast," Blue Water Woman said. "How high will this steeple of yours be?"

"As high as it needs to be for us to see out to the middle of the lake. But I would say no more than thirty feet."

Blue Water Woman stared at the chicken coop, which was eight feet high, then at the roof of their cabin. "Do you have a brain?"

"I beg your pardon?"

"You are not building a thirty-foot steeple on my roof."

"I keep telling you. It is *our* roof, and I will do as I please."

"Not if you want to share my bed, you will not."

Shakespeare stiffened, then said to Nate, "Did you hear her, Horatio? Blackmail. She thinks she can threaten me with the loss of a few cuddles." Of Blue Water Woman he demanded, "Give me one good reason why I shouldn't."

"I will give you more than one. That lumber you are using was for the storage shed you have been promising to build. The roof might not be strong enough to bear the weight of the steeple. We have bad lightning storms from time to time, and lighting likes to strike things that are up high. We have strong winds, too, and a Chinook might bring your steeple crashing down." Blue Water Woman paused in her litany. "Shall I go on?"

"Scoffs and scorns and contumelious taunts," Shakespeare quoted. "I should be angry with you if the time were convenient."

"Well?"

"Well what? Yes, we have storms, and yes, we have high winds. And soon we will have our very own steeple."

Blue Water Woman refused to let him have the final say. "If you were any more pigheaded, you would have a snout and a curly tail."

Shakespeare went to push to his feet and nearly pitched over the edge. Squatting back down, he responded, "Dwell I but in the suburbs of your good pleasure? Why must you dam the flow of my stream?"

"Oh my," Blue Water Woman said, and giggled.

At that, Nate laughed.

"Enough of this tomfoolery," Shakespeare snapped. "Go away, wench. We have a steeple and stairs to build and the day is wasting."

Blue Water Woman's grin evaporated. "What was that? No one said anything about stairs."

"How do you expect us to get up to the steeple? We can't use a ladder all the time," Shakespeare said, as he clambered higher to resume work.

"Will these stairs be inside the cabin or outside the cabin?"

"What difference does it make?"

"If they are inside, that would mean you intend to put a hole in my roof. And I will shoot you before I let that happen."

"Ye gods, woman. You could nitpick a man to death, even beyond the grave. But rest easy. The stairs will be outside, on the west end of the cabin, so we do not disturb you with our comings and goings." Shakespeare bestowed a smirk on her. "See? I can be considerate, your broadsides to the contrary."

"I think I will go visit Winona," Blue Water Woman announced. "I need a drink and we are out of brandy."

"Good riddance to you and small pox," Shakespeare shot back. "Stay most of the day if you want, and when you ride home you can admire your new steeple. It will be the envy of the neighborhood."

"I have always suspected it, but now I am sure. You are a lunatic." Blue Water Woman sniffed and raised her chin high. "I must get my shawl." She marched into the cabin.

"Women!" Shakespeare declared. "If God were not drunk when He created them, then *He* is the lunatic."

Nate lifted planks and carried them toward the ladder. "Weren't you a little hard on her?"

"Do you see these claw marks?" Shakespeare

touched his perfectly fine neck. "She came near to drawing blood. I am lucky to be alive."

"You are lucky she puts up with you."

Shakespeare aligned a nail and raised the hammer, then glanced down at Nate. "The Bard had it right when it came to women. We should all do as he says and we will have a lot less indigestion."

"What did he say?"

"Woo her, wed her, bed her, then rid the house of her."

Winona King was outside her cabin skinning a rabbit. She had caught it in a snare that morning, and by evening it would be chopped into bite-sized morsels and simmering in a stew. She loved rabbit stew. When she was little her mother had made it now and again, but nowhere near enough to suit her. Buffalo meat was their staple. They also ate venison a lot. Rabbit and other small game was resorted to only when buffalo and deer meat were not to be had.

Laying the rabbit on its back, Winona made slits down its hind legs. She peeled back the hide, slicing ligaments and muscle and scraping as required, careful to keep the edge of the knife toward the body, until she had the hide bunched around the rabbit's neck. The hide would make fine trim for a couple of her buckskin dresses.

Absorbed in her work, Winona was startled when a shadow fell across her. Her husband had gone off earlier, and her daughter was across the lake visiting Degamawaku's family.

Winona spun, her hand dropping to one of the pistols wedged under the leather belt she wore over her dress. Hostile red men and renegade whites roamed the mountains, and meat-eaters were abundant. Perils were so commonplace that she never ventured outside the cabin unarmed. Bitter experience had taught her the folly of doing so.

But now, about to unlimber a flintlock, Winona stopped with it half-drawn, and smiled.

"*Tsaangu beaichehku,*" Blue Water Woman said.

"*Tsaangu beaichehku,*" Winona said, which was Shoshone for 'Good morning.' While her friend knew some of her tongue and she knew some Salish, they usually used the language both knew almost as well as each knew her own. Decades of living under the same roof with a white man had made them fluent in the white tongue, so much so that both their husbands liked to boast they spoke English better than most whites. "This is a pleasant surprise."

"I had to get away for a while," Blue Water Woman said. "I hope you do not mind that I came here."

"Mind?" Winona said, and laughed. "You are the sister I never had. Why would I mind?"

Blue Water Woman folded her arms across her bosom and poked the ground with the toe of a moccasin. "It is that husband of mine. There are times when I want to pull out my hair."

"What has he done now?" Winona asked.

"You have not heard?" Blue Water Woman said. "He and your husband are building a steeple on our cabin."

"Nate said that he was going over to help Shakespeare with a project, but he did not—" Winona paused and blinked. "Did you say a *steeple*?"

"Yes. You have been east of the Mississippi River. You have seen the houses of worship, as whites call them, with the big bells they ring when it is time for people to come and pray and sing?"

"Their churches, yes."

"I am going to have a steeple without the church."

It made no sense to Winona. Granted, her husband was deeply religious. In the evenings, after supper, she would sit in the rocking chair and sew or knit while he would be at the table reading, and often the book he read from was the Bible. She once asked Nate if he missed going to services, and he said that while it would be nice to mix with people who shared his beliefs, his body was his temple, and the congregation consisted of him and God. He then read a passage from Scripture to that effect.

"I should be thankful," Blue Water Woman was saying, "that my idiot of a husband is not putting a bell in our steeple, or I would need to keep my ears plugged with wax."

"But why a steeple?"

"So he can keep watch for the water devil."

Winona started to laugh but caught herself. "You are serious?"

"I am afraid so." Blue Water Woman sighed. "If I live a thousand winters, I will never understand him."

"It is men," Winona said. "They do not think like we do."

"It is Shakespeare," Blue Water Woman replied. "He does not think like anyone."

Winona grinned.

"Show me one other white who spends every spare minute reading William Shakespeare or quotes him every time he opens his mouth. It is ridiculous."

"Oh my," Winona said. "If your husband ever heard you say that, he would throw a fit."

"I may throw one myself when I get home and see their steeple," Blue Water Woman said. "That is my man for you. Once he sets his mind to something, he does not rest until he has done what he set out to do. And now he has taken it into his head to go after the water devil."

"You are worried."

"I am glad Nate is helping. Shakespeare needs someone with common sense to keep an eye on him."

Ever sensitive to her friend's moods, Winona remarked, "But it is not his age that is bothering you, is it?"

"No," Blue Water Woman admitted. She gazed out over the water and bit her lower lip. "It is the water devil."

"I am sure Nate and Shakespeare will be careful," Winona sought to soothe her.

"Careful is not always enough. Some things are better left alone. A grizzly in its den. An eagle in its nest. A creature as big as a horse that lives in the water."

"In the water, yes. So long as Nate and Shakespeare stay on land, they will be safe."

"So long as they stay on land," Blue Water Woman echoed.

Steeple Knight

Shakespeare McNair would never admit it to his wife, but to him this was great fun.

Shakespeare always liked a good challenge. Throughout his life, he overcame one challenge after another and enjoyed each triumph. Add to that his love of a mystery and the fact he got to spend a lot of time in the company of the man he regarded as the son he never had, and he had a new spring in his step and a perpetual boyish grin on his wrinkled and weathered face—when he was not around Blue Water Woman.

He was not trying to deceive her in any way. He loved that woman with every particle of his being. It was just that she would never understand what the mystery of the creature in the lake meant to him.

In a way, the mystery was like that of the mountains themselves when Shakespeare first came to the Rockies all those decades ago. He was one of the first, if not *the* first, to boldly go where no white man had gone before: to venture east of the mighty Mississippi River into the unknown realm beyond.

Often, Shakespeare relived those wonderful days in his mind's eye. He saw again his first grizzly, witnessed the passage of his first nigh-endless herd of buffalo, set eyes again for the first time on the towering ramparts that would become his home for the rest of his life.

The thing in the lake was another first. It was new; it was different; it was unknown. Shakespeare had heard all the Indians' accounts. But he had never beheld any of the creatures that spawned those accounts. Now he had his chance.

Shakespeare was not one of those whites who doubted everything Indians said on general principle. Some whites refused to believe anything Indians told them simply because they *were* Indians. A prominent man of the cloth had been quoted in the newspapers as stating that those of the red race were inveterate heathens and liars. Heathens, because they did not believe in the white God. Liars, because anyone who did not believe in the white God was incapable of being true in anything.

Shakespeare had chuckled when he read it. It was just plain silly. From his own experience, Shakespeare knew that most Indians viewed with low regard anyone who talked with two tongues. Honesty and truthfulness were highly esteemed.

So when Indians told Shakespeare about the early times, about the days when the land was overrun by many strange and fearsome beasts, he listened. He had poked fun at Blue Water Woman, but he did not doubt for a minute that her tribe, and many others, believed their legends to be true, and every legend had its kernel of truth.

King Valley, as Shakespeare did not mind calling it, since Nate was the one who came up with the idea of moving there, had long been known as bad medicine by the Crows and the Utes. The valley was a throwback to the old times. It was said that *something* lived up near the glacier that fed runoff into the lake. It was also whispered that the lake itself was the haunt of *something*. Both *somethings* were said to be from the time long ago, and best avoided.

Now, after repeated puzzling and bizarre incidents, Shakespeare would very much like to know what the *something* in the lake was.

For more than a week, he and Nate kept watch from the steeple every chance they got, sometimes together, sometimes singly. They had made a bench where they could sit in relative comfort and scan the lake through Nate's spyglass.

Shakespeare was proud of the steeple. It had taken a lot of sweat to build. They only had enough planks to make it ten feet high, but combined with the height of the cabin, their new vantage afforded them a sweeping view of the lake, which was exactly what they needed.

The morning after they built it, Shakespeare took Blue Water Woman up the stairs and bid her sit on the seat and admire the view. Not only could they see more of the lake, but more of the valley, too.

Breathtaking to behold, the glory of creation unfolded before them in all its spectacular splendor.

Blue Water Woman sat and gazed quietly to the east, north, west, and south. Then she smiled in that mild manner she had, and said, "I like this. Your steeple is still silly, but I like this."

Shakespeare made a show of clearing his throat. "You made all that fuss for nothing."

"This will be a good place to come and sip tea when I want to get away from you."

Shakespeare started to laugh, then caught himself, and thought it prudent to show some indignation. "Shall quips and sentences and paper bullets of the brain awe a man from the career of his humor?"

"Do you know," Blue Water Woman said, "that I have heard there are wives whose husbands talk plainly and simply and do not quote an old, moldy book every time they open their mouth?"

"My book is not moldy!" Shakespeare took immediate offense. "This is a tale told by an idiot, full of sound and fury, signifying nothing."

Blue Water Woman smiled sweetly. "That is exactly my point."

Shakespeare could not help it; he cackled. She was the only woman he had ever met who could hold her own in banter that most women would not abide and some could not understand. The Bard, after all, was an acquired taste. Shakespeare liked to think of old William S's works as a fine wine distilled from the vineyard of the human condition. All there was to know, for those who wanted to know, could be found in the Bard's recitals of humanity's foibles and passions.

It was one of Shakespeare's great regrets that he had never made it to England. A visit to the Bard's own country would be heaven. He had it on reliable authority that people over there, by and large, adored the playwright, and read his plays for the pleasure of the reading. On the American side of the pond, William S had his partisans, but it was nothing like in Britain.

At this moment, though, seated on the bench in the steeple with the sun poised on the western brink of the world, Shakespeare was not thinking of the genius from Avon. He was scanning the lake from end to end through the spyglass. He saw fish jump. He saw ducks. He saw geese. He saw gulls. He saw a pair of red hawks. At one point a golden eagle dived and snared a fish in its great talons, then took wing again, flapping powerfully to gain altitude.

It was the eighth evening after the steeple's completion. Shakespeare had spent every minute he could on the lookout and not seen any sign of his quarry. He had begun to think that maybe his wife was right and he had gone to a lot of trouble for nothing, that perhaps their sightings of the thing would be no more frequent than before.

Then, as he was sweeping the spyglass from west to east, a tingle of excitement coursed through him.

The wind was still, the lake a mirror, its surface as calm as calm could be. But suddenly, out toward the middle, the water swelled upward as if something were pushing it from below. Shakespeare watched in fascination as the swell moved to the west, leaving broad ripples in its wake.

"I've found you, by God!" Shakespeare exclaimed. He waited with bated breath for the thing to show itself, but all he saw was the swell. After sixty or seventy feet it grew smaller and smaller until finally the lake's surface was as flat and smooth as a mirror again.

"Damn!" Shakespeare grumbled. What were they to do if the thing *never* showed itself? Some fish, after all, rarely left the depths, and when they did, they never broke the surface, but swam below it where searching eyes could not see them.

Still, Shakespeare was hopeful. He related his sighting to Nate the next day in the steeple as they sat talking over the best way to see the thing up close.

"The only way is to be out on the water when the creature comes up," Shakespeare said.

"It is too bad you and I do not have a canoe," Nate remarked. They rarely traveled by water, so he saw no need for one.

"Yes, that is too bad," Shakespeare agreed, and smiled a devious smile. "But we know someone who does."

The Nansusequas loved their new home. The tall trees, which had never been scarred by an axe, reminded them of the dense eastern woodland from which they came. The Nansusequa had always dwelled in the deep woods; it was why they called themselves the People of the Forest.

Only five escaped the massacre of their tribe. Wakumassee, the father, and Tihikanima, the mother, and their three children: Degamawaku, their son, who had been seeing a lot of Evelyn King; Tenikawaku, their oldest daughter; and Mikikawaku, their youngest.

The family always wore green. Their buckskins, their blankets, their robes—everything they owned was dyed green out of reverence for the source of the green world in which the Nansusequa lived. That Which Was In All Things, they called it, or simply the Manitoa.

On this particular morning, Wakumassee was outside their Great Lodge mending a fishing net when a clatter of hooves heralded the arrival of Shakespeare McNair on his white mare.

Waku beamed and put down the net to greet his visitor. He owed Nate King and McNair a debt impossible to repay. They had taken his family in when all was lost. They had permitted him and his loved ones to stay in the valley, safe from the whites who had slaughtered the rest of their kind.

"Welcome, friend!" Waku said. His English was not all that good, but he was working hard to master the tongue.

"Men of peace, well encountered!" Shakespeare declared, and warmly clapped him on the shoulders.

"Eh?" Wakumassee tried to sort out the words to make sense of the meaning. McNair was forever saying things that confused him. He had mentioned it once to Nate King and Nate had laughed and said not to worry, that NcNair said a lot of things that confused him, too.

"A hearty good morning to you, sirrah," Shakespeare elaborated. He regarded the net with interest. "I say. I didn't know you had one of those."

"We like to fish," Waku responded, proud he had said it as it should be said.

"I thought you were hunters."

"Hunt too," Waku said. He gestured to the east. "We fish much in rivers." He paused. "I say that right?"

"Close enough." Shakespeare squatted, set down his Hawken, gripped the net in both hands, and tugged. "This is strong enough to hold a buffalo. What is it made of?"

"Plant," Waku said. "Not know white name."

"That's all right." Chuckling, Shakespeare said, "Ask and you shall receive."

"Pardon?" Waku had learned that was the word to use when he was puzzled, and around McNair he was puzzled a lot.

"I have come to ask a favor." Shakespeare glanced at the net. "Actually, two favors."

"What I can do, I will," Waku said.

"Maybe you should hear me out," Shakespeare suggested. "It could be you don't want to."

Waku put his hand on McNair's shoulder and looked him in the eyes. "You and Nate King save us. You much kind. Give us new home. Give me hope." He struggled to find the right words. "I always your friend. Any help I can be, I do for you."

"I thank you," Shakespeare said. "I take it you have heard about my Holy Grail?"

"Pardon?"

"Perseus had the Gorgon. Theseus fought the Minotaur. St. George went up against a dragon. And now I am about to pit myself against the demon of the depths."

"Pardon?" Waku said again. He had been confused before but never *this* confused.

"Ah. Then you haven't heard. No matter." Shakespeare indicated the net. "I wonder if I might borrow that. It appears to be more than big enough for my purpose."

"Yes. Take. All I have be yours," Waku said. "You want catch fish?"

"I don't know what it is I want to catch, but I know I want to catch it, and once I catch it I will know what it is."

"Ah." Waku said, but he had no idea what the white-haired white was going on about.

"I would also like to borrow *that*," Shakespeare said, and pointed.

"Our canoe?"

"Yes." Shakespeare led the way over to the side of the Great Lodge, where the canoe sat ready to be carried to the water. Unlike the mountain tribes, who fashioned their canoes from hides or bark molded over wooden frames, the Nansusequa made their canoes using a single large log. They chipped out the center and sanded and smoothed the entire craft. The resultant dugout, while heavy and ponderous, was next to unsinkable.

"Take it," Waku said.

"I don't need the canoe right this minute," Shakespeare explained. "It might be tomorrow, it might be next week, but sooner or later I will, and I wanted to get your permission in advance."

"Take any time."

Shakespeare took Waku's hand in his. "I thank you, Wakumassee. 'Tis sweet and commendable in your nature to be so generous." He bent and lowered his voice. "One thing more, and it is important. Our arrangement is to be our little secret."

"Secret?" Waku repeated, trying to remember what the word meant.

"Yes. You are not to tell a soul."

"Not tell Nate?"

"No. He has a leaky mouth and is bound to mention it to his wife, who will run to mine to inform on me."

"You not want your wife find out?"

"Her most of all," Shakespeare said. "The Gorgon and the Minotaur were as kittens compared to her, and as for the dragon, it would call her sister."

"I not understand. But I do as you want."

Shakespeare gazed at the lake. "O monstrous beast," he quoted, "I am ready for you. Pit your wits against mine, and may the loser lead apes in hell!"

Watching and Jousting

For another week Shakespeare and Nate kept diligent watch—and saw nothing, absolutely nothing out of the ordinary. It got so Shakespeare took to pacing back and forth and muttering under his breath.

"You are letting it get to you," Nate commented late one afternoon, as he raked the lake with the spyglass. "I have not seen you this wrought up in a coon's age."

Shakespeare shook a fist in the general direction of the creature's watery realm. "I thought for sure we would have seen it a few times by now and have some idea of its habits. At the very least we should have found out whether it is a fish or something else."

"We need more time," Nate said. "More patience."

"Maybe you can afford to wait, but I can't," Shakespeare said. "As everyone keeps reminding me, I am getting on in years. I would like to find out what this thing is before I am looking up at the world through freshly dug dirt."

"You have twenty good years left in you."

"My creaking joints say different," Shakespeare said, and to get back to the issue very much on his mind, he pointed at the lake. "The thing has to have a pattern. Once we have that, we have him, her, or it, as the case may be."

"You're guessing," Nate said.

Shakespeare plopped down on the bench and shook his head. "No, I am not. Everything has its habits. Deer, bear, buffalo, birds, bugs, you name it. They do certain things in certain ways. They graze at the same time each day, or at the same place, or they wait for prey at the same spot, or visit the same patch of wildflowers."

"That is true to a point. But we are dealing with a fish."

"Are we?" Shakespeare rejoined. "We don't know what it is. But let's say you are right. Let's assume it is a fish of some kind. What do fish do? What pattern do they stick to?" He answered his own questions. "Fish swim and eat. That is pretty much it. Some, like catfish, stay down low. Bass like to stay near the shore and hide in weeds. Trout like fast-flowing streams and rivers."

"How does any of that help us with *it*?" Nate nodded at the lake.

"What do we know about it so far?" Shakespeare asked, and again answered before his friend could. "We know it is alive and big. To get that big, it had to eat a lot of whatever it eats. To stay alive, it has to go on eating. Follow me so far?"

"That is logical, yes."

"But what does it eat? Plants? I don't think so. Few fish do. Worms and bugs? Not enough of either to be had. Which tells us that the thing must eat other fish."

"Possible," Nate said.

"Probable," Shakespeare amended. "But what kind of fish? Fish near the surface or fish down deep?"

"Mostly down deep," Nate reasoned, "or we would see it near the surface more than we do."

"Good point, Horatio. So if it spends most of its time down in the depths, how are we to lure it up?"

Nate shrugged. "I am open to ideas."

"I wish I had one."

"All this talk is getting us nowhere," Nate said. He stood, gave the spyglass to Shakespeare, and moved toward the stairs. "I'd better get home. Winona will have supper on soon and she does not like it when I am late."

"Off you go, then," Shakespeare said. "Be careful not to trip over the ball and chain on your way down." He raised the spyglass to his right eye and the water came into sharp focus. Sweeping it from one end of the lake to the other, he said to himself, "Where are you, beastie? We will make you some sport if only you will show yourself."

But all Shakespeare saw was water and more water, and ducks and geese and sundry waterfowl swimming or floating or taking wing or landing. In his disgust at this state of affairs, he watched several mallards. The spyglass made it seem as if he could reach out and touch them. A male caught his interest. It was quacking up a storm. Why, he could not imagine, since the lake was as tranquil as nature allowed.

The mallard's yellow beak, the brilliant green plumage on the head, the deep chestnut brown of the front of the body, all were brought out in vivid relief by the bright rays of the setting sun.

Then suddenly the mallard was gone.

Shakespeare blinked, not sure what he had seen. One instant it had been there, quacking like crazy, the next it had disappeared under the surface. It did not dive. It did not sink. It shot straight down as if wrenched from below. He kept the telescope trained on the spot, thinking the mallard would reappear. It did not.

"There are more things in heaven and earth . . ." Shakespeare began, but he did not finish the quote. He was studying the other mallards. Most had taken wing. One female was paddling around and around near where the male had vanished. The male's mate, Shakespeare reckoned, and was touched by her devotion. Evidently ducks were not strangers to the noblest of all emotions.

Presently, the female took flight as well. But Shakespeare flattered himself that he detected a certain reluctance in her movements.

By then the sun had set, and gray twilight was spreading like a fog across the water.

Shakespeare lowered the spyglass and scratched his snowy beard. "I wonder," he said.

The next morning, the sun had not yet risen when Shakespeare climbed to the steeple. He was bundled in a heavy buffalo robe against the chill. At that altitude, even in summer, the nights could be downright cold. He had left Blue Water Woman asleep in bed. Waking her would only result in more criticism of his quest, and Shakespeare could do without that. Besides, she would be up in half an hour.

The lake lay quiet under the last of the starlight. As with most living things at that hour, the geese and ducks were silent. It was so still that a splash somewhere well out on the lake lent Shakespeare hope that at least one creature was abroad.

"Show yourself today, consarn you," Shakespeare

said to the empty air. "I defy you to prove yourself in the great heap of my knowledge."

A pink blush soon tinged the eastern horizon. On land the songbirds roused in avian chorus. Out on the water the ducks and geese stirred, their cries adding to the racket.

As soon as it was light enough, Shakespeare surveyed the lake from east to west and north to south. He saw no sign of the creature

Indulging a hunch, he concentrated on the water birds. The variety would excite a naturalist. Of ducks alone, in addition to the mallards there were buffleheads, mergansers, and goldeneyes. There were teals and grebes and coots. A few storks had shown up. Swans were conspicuous by their grace and beauty. A flock of Canadian geese were sticking close together. A killdeer had waded a short way out from shore and was giving itself a bath.

Shakespeare smiled. God, how he loved the wilderness. He could never live anywhere else, not once he had supped at the feast of nature's table and tasted of nature's many delights.

So many feathered fowl were cavorting about that Shakespeare could not make up his mind which to watch. The mallards were closer to shore than they had been the night before, and he suspected that if the thing in lake came out of the deep to partake of its breakfast, it would do so farther out.

A group of green-winged teal, with their cinnamon-red heads and rainbow-hued plumage, seemed as likely as any others, and were near the area where the male mallard had disappeared the night before. Shakespeare counted twelve, six males and six females, floating serenely.

The rising sun lent a golden glow to the lake. The light became so bright that Shakespeare had to squint against the glare. He saw the teal bob up and down on the waves, then realized, with a start of surprise, that there was no wind to speak of and the lake was virtually undisturbed. There should not be any waves.

That was when he saw it.

Something—it could well have been a giant mouth—came up out of the water and in the blink of an eye closed on one of the male teal. Before the bird could so much as lift a wing, it was swallowed whole. The rest of the teal took immediate panicked wing.

His body taut, Shakespeare raked the spot for further sign, but the thing did not reappear. After a while he stopped and leaned back with a smile. "So. Our water devil likes water fowl. Interesting."

At last Shakespeare had a tidbit of information he could use. The question was, how to use it best? He had an idea, but to put it into effect he would need Waku's canoe.

He watched the lake for another half an hour, then went down the stairs and around the cabin to the front door. The aromas that greeted him as he opened the door caused his belly to growl. "Good morning, one I love," he said cheerfully as he entered.

Blue Water Woman was fixing eggs with strips of fried venison and toast. She glanced at him, her eyes narrowing. "What is so good about it?"

Shakespeare sank into his chair and stretched his legs. "Can't a man say good morning to the other half of his heart without her being suspicious?"

"I know that tone and that look," Blue Water Woman said. "You are up to something."

"Perish forbid," Shakespeare said. "I live but to please you and wait on your every whim."

"What is the white expression?" Blue Water Woman pretended to try and remember. Suddenly she rounded on him, shaking a large wooden spoon. "You are full of it."

"Such language, madam," Shakespeare declared. "I am shocked."

"What new silliness have you cooked up?"

Shakespeare sniffed and quoted, "Were I like thee, I would throw myself away."

"Were I like you, I would need a keeper," Blue Water Woman held her own.

"Say what you will. I will no further offend you than becomes me for my good."

"So you *are* up to something," Blue Water Woman said. "And I think I know what it is."

"I say thee, ha," Shakespeare said smugly.

"I was talking to Tihikanima yesterday. She says you paid her husband a visit."

"Uh-oh."

"Strange that you never mentioned it to me. I asked her what you and Waku talked about and she said that Waku would not tell her."

"Good for him!" Shakespeare declared. "A man with backbone is worth his weight in wildcats."

"Waku also said that none of them were to use their canoe unless they checked with him first, since you might have need of it on short notice."

"Dang him. If he have wit enough to keep himself warm, let him bear it for a difference between himself and his horse."

"Now, now. Not everyone can be as sneaky as you."

"Speaking of horses, I would my horse had the speed of your tongue."

Blue Water Woman made circles in the air with the wooden spoon. "Now, what would you want with a canoe? It is too big for you to play with in the wash tub when you take your yearly bath."

"Go to, woman. Throw your vile guesses in the devil's teeth, from whence you have them."

"Funny that you should mention a devil," Blue Water Woman jousted. "And the answer is no."

"I did not realize I had asked a question," Shakespeare said, worried now.

"You intend to go out on the lake after the water devil, and I will not have it. If you will not act your age, at least respect my feelings."

"When have I ever not?" Shakespeare rallied. "And I can't catch something that lives in water if I stay on land."

"Why catch it at all?" Blue Water Woman wanted to know. "Why not let it be?"

"I would hate for a perfectly good steeple to have gone to waste."

"I am serious."

"As am I." Shakespeare thrust out his jaw in defiance. "We cannot go on living here without knowing what it is."

"Who says? We have lived here this long without knowing. You know that my people believe water devils are bad medicine. Why show them, and me, such disrespect?"

"Honest to goodness," Shakespeare said in exasperation. "Leave it to a woman to twist a man's considerate nature into an attack on her."

"Where is the consideration in you refusing to listen to me?" Blue Water Woman demanded.

"Most excellent accomplished lady," Shakespeare quoted. "The heavens rain odors on you. When did you become a tyrant?"

"I beg your pardon."

"I am old but I am not puny. I am a man, I have a will, and I will by God breathe as men breathe. If you wanted to marry a milksop you should have found a man who lets you tell him what clothes to wear."

"You are changing the subject again."

"No, I am not. The point, dearest tickle-brain, is that were a bear to come nosing around our cabin, you would have me deal with the bear. Were a fox or a coyote to become interested in our chicken coop, you would have me deal with the fox or the coyote. But let something in the lake pose a possible danger, and suddenly I am too old or too feeble or I do not respect your feelings." Shakespeare came out of his chair. "Look me in the eyes and say that again. Look into the eyes of the man who has given all that he is to make you happy and tell me I am worthless."

Blue Water Woman swallowed and averted her face. "I cannot."

"Then there will be no more talk of betrayal," Shakespeare said. "I have to do it and that is that."

"Damn you," Blue Water Woman said, but she said it softly.

"I love you, too, apple of my eye. Now how about breakfast? I cannot fight dragons on an empty stomach."

First Clash

"What do you think of our craft, Horatio?"

On his knees in the stern, Nate King smoothly stroked his paddle. He had used canoes before, in particular a Shoshone canoe that belonged to Touch the Clouds, his wife's cousin. The difference between the Shoshone canoe and the Nansusequa canoe was as night and day. The former was small and light and fast and responded superbly to every dip of the paddle; the latter was big and heavy and cumbersome, all of which combined to give it the speed and response of a brick. And because it was so heavy, the gunwales rode low to the water, barely a foot above the surface. A high wave might easily swamp them.

"I didn't hear you . . ." Shakespeare McNair prompted.

"It will do," was the best Nate could come up with.

"I think of everything, if I do say so myself," Shakespeare crowed. He indicated the net piled between them. "We should practice, so when the moment of truth comes we will be ready."

"You really expect to catch the thing with that?"

"Why else are we doing this if not to catch it and kill it?" Shakespeare responded.

Nate slowed in his stroking. "I thought you just wanted to learn what it is. What is this talk of killing?"

"Since when do you mind getting rid of an animal that could prove a menace?" Shakespeare rejoined. "You killed that grizzly, remember? And we had to make worm food of those wolverines."

"The griz tried to break into our cabin, and those wolverines were out for our blood," Nate noted. "I have no quarrel with this water devil, or whatever it is."

"You will change your mind. Wait and see." Shakespeare scanned the lake. They were drawing near where the mallard and the teal had been taken.

"I had no idea you were so bloodthirsty," Nate teased. Only, now that he thought about it, he recalled that McNair had urged him to slay the grizzly the day they arrived in the valley. Other instances came to mind, leading him to say, "You like to nip danger in the bud, is that it?"

"In a manner of speaking," Shakespeare admitted. He knew of too many men and women, red and white, who had lost their lives because they did not take a threat seriously enough.

"The water devil does not need nipping," Nate said. "The thing never comes up on land. We have nothing to worry about."

"We don't know that it always stays in the water," Shakespeare pointed out. "We *assume* it does."

"If it's a fish, we leave it alone."

Shakespeare twisted to look at him. "Where is your sense of adventure? Of sport?"

"I only kill when I have to," Nate·said. "To feed my family or protect them, or to defend myself."

"You have never hunted for hunting's sake?"

Nate answered honestly. "When I was younger, yes, but only a few times." He was well aware that most men did not share his view. Most liked to hunt and fish for the challenge and the thrill. He suspected he had his mother to thank for his outlook; she would never harm so much as a fly.

"What do these feathered yacks think they are doing?" Shakespeare wondered.

A dozen buffleheads had swum into their path. Shakespeare applied his paddle to veer the dugout around them, but it was slow to respond. Fortunately, the nervous buffleheads swam faster. He waited until the canoe was clear to say, "I have hunted since I was old enough to hold a gun and fished since I was old enough to swing a pole. To me this critter is no different than any other. I aim to catch it, come what may."

"If you ask me—" Nate began, and stopped. To their north, perhaps forty feet away and just under the surface, something was moving. Something big. He pointed and exclaimed, "Do you see what I see?"

"By my troth!" Shakespeare blurted. Thanks to the play of the bright sunlight on the surface and the dark murk below, he could not be entirely sure of what he was seeing.

"Is that the thing we are after?"

"There is only one way to find out," Shakespeare said, and sheared his paddle so the canoe swung toward it. He had brought the spyglass, but it was under his buckskin shirt, and anyway, another half dozen strokes and they would be near enough to have a good look. "Faster!" he urged, stroking harder.

"Maybe we shouldn't get too close," Nate cautioned.

"Nonsense." Shakespeare leaned forward, eager for a better look. But the creature was no longer there. He stopped paddling and looked on both sides of the canoe, but it was gone. "Damnation!"

Secretly, Nate was glad. He was worried his friend might draw a pistol and shoot the thing.

"Where in blazes did it get to?" Shakespeare leaned farther out. The sunlight penetrated about six feet down. Below that lay the shadowy realm of the unknown.

"Off to take a nap."

Shakespeare ignored the barb. He had a new habit of dozing off after big meals. Eating brought on a lassitude he could not shake. "If you are going to pick at me with your bowie, the least you could—" He abruptly stopped.

Down in the dark, something had moved. A giant shape was almost directly below them and rising fast.

"There!" Shakespeare cried.

"Paddle!" Nate shouted. He did so, but he had only stroked twice before the canoe gave a violent lurch and lifted half a foot out of the water. Grabbing the sides, he clung on as the canoe smacked back down with a loud *whomp* and water splashed in.

The creature promptly disappeared.

"Did you see him, Horatio!" Shakespeare said, laughing in delight. "Did you see the size of him?"

Nate had seen little beyond the suggestion of great bulk. "We need to get out of here."

"No! It might come back."

"That's what I am afraid of." Nate peered down, and sure enough, the bulk was rising toward them again. "It is going to hit us again!"

The next instant the creature did just that, this time striking the bow. Shakespeare grabbed hold of the prow as the canoe once again canted up out of the water and came smashing down with a gigantic splash.

The creature was already gone.

Nate could not get out of there fast enough. He worked his paddle furiously, then saw that instead of helping, Shakespeare was laughing. "We need to *go*! We need to go *now*!"

Still shaking with mirth, Shakespeare said, "Be at ease, Horatio. The canoe is too heavy to tip over. We are safe enough."

"Like hell," Nate said. He had the impression that the creature had not really tried to upend them. So far. "You might have a death wish, but I do not. Paddle, consarn you!"

"You would worry a wart to death," Shakespeare said, and reluctantly dipped his paddle.

Nate chafed at how slowly the canoe turned. Once the bow was pointed toward shore, he pumped his arms, spray flying from under his paddle. McNair, however, was more intent on peering over the sides and only half exerting himself.

"Why am I doing all the work?"

"Because I have yet to get a good look at it," Shakespeare said. "And unlike you, I have not yellowed my britches."

"It's only common sense," Nate said angrily.

An unusual sound behind them, a sibilant sort of hiss that reminded Nate of nothing so much as the hiss of a snake, made him snap his head around. Sixty feet out, and closing, was a growing swell such as they had occasionally witnessed from shore. "It's after us!"

Shakespeare swiveled, and cackled. "I do believe it is! What a stroke of luck!"

"Did you leave your common sense at home today?" Nate asked, applying himself to his paddle with renewed vigor. "Help, damn it!"

"Mercy me, the language you use!" Shakespeare said, but he bent to his paddle with a strength uncommon for someone who had seen as many years as he had.

"I did not count on this!" Nate said. He'd figured the creature, whatever it was, would fight shy of them. But not only was it not scared of them, twice it had bumped them from below, and now it appeared to be bearing down on them with the clear intent of ramming the dugout.

Shakespeare's grin faded. He had not counted on this, either. Here he had been trying for days to come up with a way to lure the thing to them, and it had proven ridiculously easy. All they had to do was venture out on the lake. *Getting back to land* now posed the problem. His cockiness to the contrary, they were at a severe disadvantage. Their adversary was in its natural element; they were out of theirs. It did not help that their canoe was as slow as molasses.

The hissing grew louder.

Nate glanced over his shoulder. The swell was only thirty feet away, and closing. The water the creature displaced, cascading over its huge form, was the source of the hissing. "It's gaining!"

Shakespeare could see that for himself. As big and heavy as the canoe was, the creature was bigger and likely heavier. If it should strike them at full speed, the result would not be pleasant. He glued his eyes to the swell, and when it was only six feet from the stern, he bawled, "To the right, Horatio! Swing us out of its way!"

Nate exerted every sinew in his body. The hissing

became even louder, eclipsing all sound except the hammering of his heart. He nearly whooped for joy when the dugout angled to one side and the swell went hurtling past.

"We did it!" Shakespeare shouted.

Nate yipped in delight.

But their elation proved premature.

The swell subsided as the creature began to submerge. But just when it appeared the thing would sink out of sight and go on its way, the leading edge of the swell began to turn, and as it turned, it grew in size.

"It's circling back at us!" Nate exclaimed.

Shakespeare experienced a twinge of regret. He would hate for Nate to come to harm when it had been his brainstorm to come out after the thing. He suspected Nate had tagged along more out of concern for him than from an abiding interest in the creature.

"Paddle harder!"

Shakespeare shifted. *God in heaven, the thing is fast!* It would be on them in no time. He stroked his paddle like a man possessed.

Nate was doing the same.

The shore was impossibly far away. They would never reach it in time. Desperate to keep from being rammed, Shakespeare stopped paddling and swooped his hand to his waist.

"What are you doing?"

Shakespeare did not answer. He whipped out a flintlock and thumbed back the hammer. He aimed for the front of the swell, for where he figured the creature's head would be.

Nate froze with his paddle partway raised. A 'No!' was on the tip of his tongue, but he did not give voice to the shout.

Shakespeare fired. At the blast the pistol spewed smoke and lead. He thought he saw the slug strike the water. But the swell—and the creature—kept coming. He grabbed for his other pistol, determined to stop it if he could. As his fingers wrapped around the hardwood, a miracle occurred: the swell changed direction and passed within spitting distance of their canoe.

Nate was mesmerized. He longed to see the creature clearly, but all he saw was moving water and a dark silhouette. He caught sign of a fin, or imagined he did, and then the thing was past and the swell was rapidly dwindling as its source dived for the depths. The hissing faded. In seconds there was nothing to mark the creature's passage beyond ripples and a few frothy bubbles.

"That was close," Shakespeare said, exhaling in relief.

"You wounded it or scared it off," Nate said, grateful whichever the case might be.

"Did you get a good look at it?"

"No. Did you?"

"Would that I had."

"All that we just went through and we still have no idea what we are up against."

"If it had struck us . . ." Nate let the statement dangle.

"Our broken bodies would have washed up on shore in a day or two and my wife would get to tell mine she told me so," Shakespeare said with a grin. Sobering, he lowered the pistol he had not realized he was still pointing at the water. "Do you still doubt that it is dangerous?"

"It can be," Nate allowed. "But so long as we stay off the lake, we should be fine."

"Then I take it you are going to ride over to Waku's and tell him and his family they can't fish anymore. And after that, you will go over to your son's and inform Zach and Lou that there will be no more swimming or bathing in the lake. Winona and Evelyn will need to—"

"I get the point," Nate broke in.

"So what will it be? Do we let the critter alone, or do we make the lake safe for us and our kin? What wouldst thou of us, Trojan?"

"I am from Troy now?"

Shakespeare quoted, "A true knight, not yet mature, yet matchless; firm of word, speaking in deeds, and deedless in his tongue; not soon provoked, nor being provoked soon calmed." He paused. "Have you been provoked, sir? Is it war or is it peace?"

"It is war," Nate King said.

The King Valley Water Devil Society

"What are you up to, wench?"

Blue Water Woman gave her husband an innocent look and said, "I have no idea what you mean."

"From the extremist upward of thy head to the descent and dust below thy foot, a most toad-spotted traitor," Shakespeare quoted.

"You think that you know what this is about?"

"Methink'st thou art a general offense and every man should beat thee," Shakespeare said testily.

The sun was low in the western sky, and they were making their way along the shore toward the King cabin. At Blue Water Woman's insistence they were walking instead of riding. Shakespeare did not mind, as it was not far, and it was good to have ground under his feet after his harrowing experience on the lake. He happened to gaze to the northwest and noticed two people in the distance approaching hand in hand along the west shore.

"What's this? Zach and Lou are on their way to Nate's, too? Did Winona invite them as well?"

"All I know," Blue Water Woman said, "is that she invited us to supper. Beyond that, your guess, as whites like to say, is as good as mine."

"You speak with a forked tongue, woman," Shakespeare grumbled. "You are up to something. You and Winona both. But I am telling you in advance that whatever it is, it won't work."

"My, my," Blue Water Woman said. "We can add predicting the future to your many talents."

"More of your conversation would infect my brain," Shakespeare quoted. He had more to say, but just then he glanced over his shoulder and beheld five figures in green hurrying along the water's edge from the east. "Look yonder. Waku and his family are coming, too." He glared at his wife. "What is this? You and Winona have invited everyone in the valley."

"It is their home as well as ours," Blue Water Woman said. "They should take part in important matters."

"Aha!" Shakespeare erupted, pointing a finger at her. "I knew it! Blasts and fogs upon thee!"

"I like fog," Blue Water Woman teased. "Walking in it is like walking in a cloud."

"You are not worth the dust which the rude wind blows in your face."

"And you would know about wind, one I love, as you are as big a bag of air as any man ever born."

Shakespeare nearly tripped over his own feet in his surprise. It was rare for her to thrust so directly. "Well now. So it is pistols at twenty paces. But in a battle of wits I am taking advantage of you, as you are unarmed."

"A fool go with thy soul, whither it goes."

Shakespeare stopped cold. "My God. You just quoted the Bard to *me*?"

"I have not lived with you all these winters, listening to you recite him day in and day out, without picking up a few of his sayings."

"That was beautiful. Do that tonight under the sheets and I will show you why they call me Carcajou."

"You are hopeless," Blue Water Woman said, and walked on.

Evelyn King was waiting to greet them. She hugged Blue Water Woman and pecked Shakespeare on the cheek. "Ma had me wait out here to welcome everyone. This will be fun. We haven't had everyone all together in a spell."

"Why did your mother ask us here?" Shakespeare inquired.

"You will have to wait and find out with the rest," Evelyn said, and gave his hand a tender squeeze. "She told me to say that. She said you would pester me if I didn't."

"Females! Their tongues outvenom all the worms of the Nile."

"I am a female, Uncle Shakespeare."

"Yes, girl. But you are young and innocent yet. Deceit has not found lodgement in your veins."

"Are you saying that all females are deceitful?"

"Never in a million years, child. Only those who live and breathe."

Blue Water Woman smiled wearily at Evelyn. "You must forgive him. When he was an infant he was dropped on his head."

Evelyn laughed cheerfully. "I love how you two can poke fun at one another and not get mad."

"He does most of the poking," Blue Water Woman said.

Shakespeare wondered if she meant what he thought she meant. For all her meekness, her wit was every whit as sharp as his, and she was not above thrusting deep when the occasion called for it.

Coughing, he said, "How about if we go on in? I would like to find out what all this is about."

"Go ahead," Evelyn said, "but the finding out will have to wait."

"Why?"

"I heard Ma tell Pa that she wants everyone here before she explains why she and Blue Water Woman called us all together."

"My wife, you say?" Shakespeare said, and gave his other half a smug glance. "If I were any brighter I would be the sun."

"I sometimes think that in a past life you must have been a rooster," was Blue Water Woman's retort.

"A noble bird. I commend your choice."

"Yes, roosters like to preen and strut and crow."

"I am twice pricked," Shakespeare said. He placed a hand on his hunting knife. "Want me to give this to you so you can do it right?"

Squealing with glee, Evelyn clapped her hands as if she were applauding a play on a stage. "Oh! Keep it up! It gives me something to write about in my diary."

Just then five figures in green came around the corner. Wakumassee and his wife, Tihikanima, were in the lead. After them came Degamawaku, their oldest, then their daughters, Tenikawaku and Mikikawaku.

"Dega!" Evelyn exclaimed, and dashed to meet him.

"Strange how of the five she only has eyes for one," Shakespeare playfully remarked.

"As you said, she is young yet," Blue Water Woman responded. "She has not learned that men are fickle in their affection and do not care if they cause unending worry for those who care for them."

Shakespeare was spared another round by the arrival of Zach and Lou. He shook hands and they all went in.

Nate was at the counter, sipping coffee. He raised his cup in greeting. "Take a seat, everyone. My wife will be with us directly."

The table and chairs had been pushed against a wall so there was space for everyone to sit on the floor. Shakespeare eased down and crossed his legs, his elbows on his knees. "Do you know what this is about, Stalking Coyote?" he asked Zach, using the younger man's Shoshone name.

"All my mother would tell me when she rode over to invite us was that we must be here on time."

Louisa was grinning from ear to ear. "We should do this once a month for the fun of it. We don't see everyone often enough."

The bedroom door opened and out came Winona. She had on her usual beaded buckskin dress and moccasins. *"Tsaangu yeitabai'yi.* Good afternoon, and welcome. I am glad all of you could make it," she said in flawless English. She was a natural linguist; every language she learned, she learned well. Only Shakespeare spoke more tongues, and then only because he had lived so much longer and been acquainted with various tribes in his travels.

"I am surprised you and my wife didn't invite the Shoshones and the Flatheads while you were at it," he now remarked.

"Pay him no mind," Blue Water Woman said. "He is in one of his moods."

"I blush to think upon this ignomy," Shakespeare muttered.

"Don't start."

"Since most of us speak English, I will use that tongue," Winona announced. Turning to her Nansusequa guests, she addressed Wakumassee and Degamawaku. "You two speak it the best in your family, but you are still learning. I will talk slowly and use small words so you can translate for the others."

"I am speaking the white tongue good," Dega declared, proud of his accomplishment. That he had extra incentive in the form of Evelyn King was not a fact he mentioned.

"You have improved a lot since we met," Winona agreed. "But I will still speak slowly so it is easy for you to translate." She raised her arms to get everyone's attention. "The first ever meeting of the King Valley Water Devil Society is now in session."

Shakespeare sat up. "The what?"

"The King Valley Water Devil Society. Do you like the name? Blue Water Woman came up with it."

"I should have known."

"What be society?" Wakumassee asked. "That one I not know."

"It was a little jest on my part," Winona explained.

"A tiny jest is more like it," Shakespeare said under his breath, but loud enough for everyone to hear. "Why beat around the bush? You called this meeting because you and my wife are worried."

"We have reason to be," Winona said. "We were in the steeple today. We saw what happened."

Nate put his cup down. "You never mentioned anything to me."

Shakespeare frowned at his wife. "All your squawking about the steeple being a waste of wood and you go up there to spy on us?"

"If caring for someone and wanting to be sure

they are not harmed is spying, then yes, we were spying."

"I was right about you being up to something," Shakespeare said.

"Yes, you were right. We talked it over in the steeple and decided to call this meeting."

"Say that again."

"Excuse me?"

"That part about me being right. In front of witnesses, no less." Shakespeare made a show of looking at the ceiling and then out the window. "I expect the world to end any moment."

"Who say world end?" Waku asked in some alarm. "Nansusequa believe world stay as is until moon fall down."

Louisa piped up with, "How is that again?"

"You might as well say the world will end when there are no more buffalo," Zach threw in.

Nate came over and put one of his big hands on Winona's slender shoulder. "It is not like you to keep secrets. Why didn't you say something?"

"I am now."

"Fine," Shakespeare said in disgust. "Horatio can stay home from now on. But I am not giving up. I will go out on the lake by myself if I have to. That thing must be dealt with."

"I agree," Winona said.

"So what if I am the only one who—" Shakespeare stopped abruptly. "What did you just say?"

"I agree with you. It could have been anyone out there today. Waku and Dega, fishing. Or my cousin when he pays a visit. Or one of us ladies out for a swim." Winona shook her head. "Until today the water devil has been no more than a nuisance. Now I fear it could well kill one of us."

"I think the same," Blue Water Woman said.

Shakespeare sat back, unable to hide his astonishment. "Let me get this straight. When I was going on about how we had to do something and built the steeple, you flayed me hour by hour. But as soon as Winona says we need to act, you are all for it."

"I did not change my mind because of Winona," Blue Water Woman said. "I changed it because I saw the water devil try to kill you."

Deeply touched but refusing to show it, Shakespeare coughed and asked, "Aren't you forgetting the bad medicine?"

"If there is no creature, there is no bad medicine."

Nate studied his wife, "I am happy you have come over to our way of thinking. But why did you invite everyone here?"

"I have been wondering the same thing," Zach said. "You could have told us all this tomorrow."

"True," Winona acknowledged. "If that was all there is to it. But when I called this the King Valley Water Devil Society, I was not joking. This valley is our home. We have chosen to spend our lives here. We must make it as safe as we can."

"My exact sentiments," Shakespeare said.

"After what we saw," Winona said, "it is clear the two of you can use help."

Shakespeare took immediate exception. "I wouldn't say that. We need to plan better, is all."

"Again, I agree."

"Keep this up and I will think I am drunk. Which is some feat, given that I have not tasted liquor in a month."

"I was not finished," Winona said. "This should not be on your shoulders alone."

"Hostiles, bears, and monsters are man's work."

Blue Water Woman snorted.

"All of us have a stake," Winona went on. "We must plan together and work together to rid the lake of the water beast."

"I suppose you have worked out exactly how we should go about it?" Shakespeare said, with a trace of mockery.

"Blue Water Woman and I have come up with an idea that should work, yes."

"I am all ears."

"The easiest way to catch an animal is to set a trap for it. All you need is the right bait."

"And what sort of bait do you reckon will bring that thing up out of the depths?" Shakespeare asked.

Both Winona and Blue Water Woman looked at him and grinned.

The Armada

There were as many ways to make canoes as there were tribes to make them. Some did as the Nansusequa liked to do and hollowed out logs. Some built frames and covered them with hide. Others preferred bark. Nate King had even heard of a tribe that used planks and sealed the gaps between the planks with pitch.

Some tribes were partial to large canoes, other tribes only used small ones, and then there were those that relied on both. Some liked the sides of their canoes to be high to ward off enemy arrows and lances. Others constructed canoes that sat low in the water so it was easier to fish.

Even the shapes of the canoes varied. Certain tribes liked the ends to come to points. Others preferred rounded ends. Still others chose square ends.

All this came up in the days that followed the meeting. Winona and Blue Water Woman insisted more canoes be made. As Winona summed up their sentiments, "If the water devil had capsized your dugout, we would have had no way of reaching you in time to help."

It was decided they needed at least four craft besides the one they had. Nate was put in charge of building what Shakespeare took to calling their armada. The Nansusequa offered to hollow out more logs, but Nate and Shakespeare tactfully suggested that smaller, lighter craft might be better. After their experience with the dugout, they would be damned, as Shakespeare put it, if they "ever used one of those floating death traps again. The only thing it has to commend it is that it can be chopped up and used for firewood."

That left them the choice of hide canoes or bark canoes. Birch bark was highly touted, but the valley did not have many birch trees. Ash was a good substitute, but it would take hours to reach the nearest stand.

"Hide canoes will be easier to make than bark and less likely to sink," suggested Nate.

"I am all for staying dry," Shakespeare said.

The valley teemed with game, and they were experts at skinning and tanning. Shakespeare wanted to use deer hides since "there are so many damn deer, we trip over them every time we step out the door." Initially, Nate disagreed. He thought elk hides would be better. But the elk were high up at that time of year, and when he factored in the time it would take to ride up into the high country after them and come back again, he went along with McNair.

"Deer it is."

Over the next several days, the valley resounded with the boom of rifles. Nate, Shakespeare, and Zach all went deer hunting. After each deer was slain, they would tote it on a pack horse to the lake where the women and the Nansusequas took over.

At one point, Winona remarked to Louisa that she was surprised Lou had not gone with the men, as she loved to hunt as much as Zach did.

Lou looked down at her belly and replied, "I just don't feel up to it." She did not elaborate.

In Winona's estimation, the women had the harder job. Skinning, curing, and tanning a hide took three days, and they had a lot of hides to prepare.

The skinning went smoothly, so long as the animal was freshly killed. The hides peeled off with little effort, much like the skin of the banana Winona once had when she visited the States.

Next came the soaking. All the hides had to be immersed in water for half a day. It softened them and made them pliable. Usually Winona soaked her hides in a large wooden tub, but since they had so many to get ready and they did not want to be all month at it, she proposed soaking them in the lake. They waded out until the water came to their knees, then weighed the hides down with rocks.

While the hides soaked, they fashioned frames for the stretching and fleshing.

At the end of half a day, each hide was taken from the water and wrung out. Then the hide was attached to the frame using cords spaced about a hand's width apart around the outer edge.

Fleshing involved scraping away the fat and tendons. It was tedious work, but essential. Normally, they would also remove the hair, but since these particular hides would not be made into clothes and the hair would make the hides more resistant to water, it was left on.

Evelyn was put in charge of boiling the deer brains. She did not care for the task. The feel of holding a brain always made her vaguely queasy. But she did not complain.

Evelyn would crack the skulls and scoop out the brains. She then placed them in a pot over a fire, and once the water was at full boil, she took them out and put them in cool water for a while. Usually they were still warm when she picked them out of the cool water and worked them with her fingers to get rid of the membranes.

Finally, Evelyn gave the brains to Tihikanima and her daughters, and they rubbed the brains on the sides of the hides that did not have hair. They rubbed and rubbed until the brains were the consistency of paste.

Afterward, the hides were placed in the shade for another half a day, then soaked again. To further waterproof them, they were hung on a tripod over a fire and smoked.

All that was only the beginning.

The men built the frames, but it was the women who fitted the hides over them. It had to be done hair side out, with the women exercising great care that they did not accidentally puncture or cut each hide.

Twelve days after the meeting, they had their armada: four deer-hide canoes, in addition to the log canoe that Waku and Dega insisted on using.

It was a proud moment when they lined up the canoes on the shore and stood admiring their handiwork.

Shakespeare sobered them by shaking a fist at the lake and hollering, "We are coming for you, beast! It is either you or us and it will by God not be us!"

"I wish you had not put it that way," Nate said.

"Your problem, Horatio," Shakespeare responded, "is that you like your reality to be worry free."

"I am not an infant."

"I am only saying that we go from the cradle to the grave under the double grindstone of uncertainty and toil, and no amount of wishful thinking will change that."

"Talk about a cheerful outlook," Nate said.

The time had come.

The canoes, the paddles, the net, the special weapons—everything was ready.

They knew the creature fed at daybreak; Shakespeare had seen the teal taken with his own eyes. The next dawn found them on the west shore, preparing to launch their armada.

Nate and Shakespeare both had canoes to themselves. In the third came Winona and Blue Water Woman. Zach and Lou had the fourth. Last to launch were Waku and Dega in the dugout.

Evelyn, Tihikanima, and the Nansusequa girls stayed on shore.

Zach King was glad his sister was not going. She had wanted to, but their parents had insisted she stay behind. Zach was not so glad about Lou tagging along. He could not bear the thought of harm befalling her. It was bad enough she had been acting strangely of late; she was often withdrawn and distracted, and a moment of distraction out on the lake could have dire consequences.

Now, stroking powerfully, Zach looked back at her. "Are you all right?"

"Yes. Why do you ask?" Lou absently replied while matching her rhythm to his.

"You looked a little peaked when you woke up."

"It's nothing."

"Maybe you should have stayed in bed," Zach said. "I can manage on my own."

"It's nothing!" Lou repeated irritably. She had not told him about her queasiness.

"I can take you back to shore," Zach offered, hiding his surprise. She was rarely cross with him without cause.

"I am fine, I tell you." But Lou did not feel fine. The motion of the canoe was doing unpleasant things to her stomach. She closed her eyes for a bit, and when she opened them again she felt a little better.

Over in his canoe, Nate King overheard their exchange and did not like it. He remembered the romantic tryst they had taken up to the glacier a while back, with the express aim of starting a family, and he marveled that Louisa had not put two and two together. Increasing his speed, Nate brought his canoe alongside McNair's. In his haste, they nearly collided.

"What the blazes?" Shakespeare exclaimed. "If you are trying to send me to the bottom, you are off to a good start."

Nate gazed about to be sure no one would hear and said quietly, "I think Louisa is pregnant."

"She isn't sure yet," Shakespeare replied.

"You knew about it?"

"I know everything."

"Why didn't you say something? She is my daughter-in-law."

"Didn't you hear me say she isn't sure yet? I will be happy to tell you when she is."

"You are particular about your gossip. That is rare for a biddy hen."

Shakespeare snorted like a incensed bull. "You prattle something too wildly, Horatio." He regarded the canoe bearing Zach and Lou. "If she is, she should not be with us, but since she is here, we must take special care she is not placed in harm's path."

Nate nodded. They had already decided that when

the creature was sighted, Zach and Lou were to move in close and while Lou handled the paddle, Zach would cast one of their special weapons. "I will go in first when we spot the thing instead of them, Nate said."

"Why you and not me?" Shakespeare demanded.

"I said it first."

"I was born first."

"That's a ridiculous reason." Nate used his paddle. "I will go tell Zach and Louisa."

"Don't let on why."

Nate angled his canoe to intercept his son and daughter-in-law. They were so intent on the water ahead that they did not notice him until he was almost on them. "There's been a change in plans."

"Pa?"

"You and Lou will hang back and help Waku and Dega with the net."

"But we already talked it out. I want in on the kill," Zach reminded him.

"Be ready in case we miss." Nate paddled away to avoid being quizzed. His son sounded disappointed, and he did not blame him. All Zach's life, he had lived for the thrill of counting coup and the challenge of the hunt. Then Zach married Lou, and her love had blunted his bloodletting. But deep down Zach was still Zach; he still relished the excitement of pitting himself against any and all comers.

Soon they were well out on the lake. The sun was half up, casting the sky in hues of yellow and pink. The waterfowl were astir. Ducks quacked and flapped, swans arched their long necks and raised their large wings, gulls squawked in raucous irritation. A pair of storks winged in low and alighted with admirable grace given their ungainly appearance. Fish were beginning to jump.

Nate straightened and scanned the lake from end to end. If Shakespeare was right, the thing would soon rise out of the depths to feed. They must be ready, or they would miss the chance. He checked on the others. Winona and Blue Water Woman were to his right, Shakespeare to his left, the others trailing.

Once the creature was sighted, Winona and Blue Water Woman would swing to the north of it, Shakespeare to the east, Zach and Lou and the Nansusequa to the west, and Nate to the south.

"We will surround the varmint," Shakespeare had proposed. "The only way it can escape us will be straight down."

Now, Nate stopped paddling and placed the paddle crosswise across the gunwales. The smell of the water, the lap of the wavelets against the canoe, and the shrieks of the gulls brought to vivid mind his last encounter. He hoped to God they fared better this time.

Nate did not like having the women along. Not because he felt he was any better at handling a canoe, or any tougher, or even because he was a man and they were women. He did not want them there because he cared dearly for them, and what they were doing was terribly dangerous. He gazed across at Winona and Blue Water Woman. Winona noticed he was looking at them, and smiled and called out.

"Is everything all right?"

With a lump in his throat, Nate smiled and nodded.

"Be careful, husband."

"You too, wife."

The part of the lake in their vicinity was still and serene. A few geese were to the southeast.

Closer were nine mergansers, the males black and white, the females a dusky gray. The flock swam past Winona's canoe without breaking formation, their heads held high, their tails twitching.

Nate glanced down at the special weapons in the bottom of his canoe. Shakespeare had insisted that one weapon was not enough, so each canoe had a pair. He fingered one, praying his cast would be true.

The mergansers started making a racket.

Tensing, Nate looked up. The surface showed no sign of a disturbance below.

Squawking louder, the mergansers broke rank.

"What's going on?" Louisa wondered.

Suddenly the mergansers scattered. Several frantically flapped their wings to get airborne.

That was when the monster struck.

Disaster

They all saw it.

One of the mergansers was starting to rise into the air, its webbed feet brushing the surface, when the lake bulged upward. The merganser uttered a sharp *karr-karr-karr*, its wings flapping furiously. In the blink of an eye it was gone, not so much as a feather to mark its demise.

His every nerve tingling, Nate King, who was nearest, paddled swiftly toward the spot.

Other mergansers gained altitude. Those that had not taken to the air were streaking through the water with fear-induced speed, their heads thrust forward, raising their cries to the sky.

A female was swimming in panicked flight directly toward the canoe Winona and Blue Water Woman were in. The terrified duck did not seem to see them. Both women were frozen by the tableau, their paddles in their hands.

Nate probed the water for the creature, but the glare of the rising sun hid whatever lay below.

Suddenly the female merganser, now only thirty feet from Winona and Blue Water Woman, let out with a *karr-karr-karr* of her own. The next moment she was wrenched under and was gone.

"Look out!" Shakespeare shouted.

A swell was rising in the spot where the duck had disappeared. As before, all that could be seen was the vaguest outline of a huge shape. With alarming rapidity, the creature bore down on Winona and Blue Water Woman's canoe.

"Ma!" Zach hollered, and worked his paddle to go to her aid. Louisa immediately did the same.

Nate was using his own with all the might in his muscles. He saw Winona reach down for one of their special weapons, but before she could lift it and just when it appeared certain the creature was going to ram them, the swell shrank and the creature passed under them. The swell reappeared on the other side and began to circle the canoes.

Relief coursed through Nate. If anything had happened to his wife——he could not finish the thought. She was everything to him. Were she to die, he would never recover, never be the same. Some losses were too horrible to be borne.

Zach stopped paddling now that his mother was safe, and Lou took her cue from him.

"That was close," she said.

"Too close," Zach agreed. He glanced at his father and then toward Shakespeare, who yelled something Zach did not quite catch, and jabbed an arm as if pointing at something.

"Zachary?" Lou said uneasily.

"What is it?" Zach responded, looking in the direction that Shakespeare was pointing.

"Dear God!" Lou said.

Zach rarely felt fear. Even in the frenzied heat of battle, he was always able to keep his wits about him and not succumb to fright. But he felt it now, a spike of raw, pure, potent fear that gripped his chest in a fist of ice.

The thing was coming toward them.

Louisa asked anxiously, "What do we do? Hope it goes under us, or get out of its way?"

Zach did not know. They could not outrun it. It moved three times as fast as they could ever hope to propel the canoe. And if they started to turn, it might ram them broadside. For a few seconds he was paralyzed with indecision, and then his instincts took over. He had one unfailing response to being attacked: he killed the attacker. Whether human or animal, it made no difference. If someone or something attacked him or a loved one, that someone or something died. It was as simple as that.

Nate and Winona added their shouts of warning to Shakespeare's, Nate's the loudest.

"Use a harpoon!"

Zach glanced down. It had been McNair's idea to make them. As Shakespeare had put it when he brought it up at the meeting, "We shot the thing and it had no effect. It is so big we can't be sure where its vitals are. So I propose we build us a bunch of harpoons."

"Harpoons?" Dega had repeated quizzically.

"Whites use them to kill critters called whales," Shakespeare had explained. "Whales look like fish but they are as big as this cabin, or bigger."

"How whites kill?" Waku had asked.

"We go after them in boats and throw harpoons into them with ropes tied to the end, so if they try to get away they pull the boats after them."

"But what be harpoon?" Waku was still confused.

"Think of it as a lance, only bigger and thicker.

The tips are made of metal and stick in the whale and won't come out."

Now, with the swell sweeping toward him and his wife, Zach reached down and grabbed a harpoon. Over seven feet long and made of pine, it was as thick as his forearm. He had to use both hands to throw it. One end had been sharpened and then charred in a fire so it was rock-hard, the other had a hole in it.

Remembering Shakespeare's instruction, Zach bent and snatched up the rope that was coiled in the bow. Quickly, he went to thread the rope through the hole. But he was not given the time.

"*Zachary!*" Lou cried.

The thing was almost on top of them.

The hiss of water was loud in Zach's ears as he rose on his knees and raised the harpoon aloft. He could not see the creature, but he had a fair notion of where it was, and without hesitation he let his harpoon fly. The tip sliced into the swell about where the thing's head would be, or so Zach hoped.

But nothing happened. The creature kept coming. The lance was swept aside by the rushing water and bobbed up and down in the wake.

"Damn!" Zach reached for the second harpoon. Up to the very last instant he thought the thing might pass under their canoe as it has passed under Winona and Blue Water Woman's.

Then the creature slammed into them.

Lou screamed and clutched at the sides of the canoe. The bow swept upward and the whole craft tilted. Zach reached for her, and she lunged for his arms. But before she could grab hold, the canoe rolled.

Louisa gasped as cold water enveloped her, and in gasping, she swallowed water. Clamping her mouth shut, she tried to hold her breath, but there was no breath to hold.

Zach, tumbling, felt a blow to his side, then a scraping sensation and pain. He tumbled end over end, water getting into his nose and ears but not his mouth. He'd had the presence of mind to suck in a breath of air in the split second before he went under.

Dimly, Zach was conscious of a great bulk sweeping by him. He glimpsed a silhouette: a narrow head, an enormous arched body, what might be fins or a tail. Then the thing was gone, and he kicked toward the lighter water above. Breaking the surface, he turned this way and that, seeking his wife. Nearby, the canoe floated on its side but was slowly sinking.

A shadow fell across him. Zach twisted as immensely powerful hands gripped him by the shoulders and started to lift him out of the water. "No, Pa. Not yet."

"We have to get you out of the water," Nate said.

"No!" Zach glanced wildly about. "Where's Louisa? Lou! *Lou!*"

From all quarters help was coming: Shakespeare, paddling like mad from the east; Winona and Blue Water Woman, their faces grim; Waku and Dega with their slow-as-a-turtle log dugout.

But otherwise the lake was undisturbed. The swell was gone. The creature was gone. And so was Louisa.

"Dear God," Zach said, and dived. He reasoned that she had to be somewhere close, unless the thing had caught her in its jaws and carried her off. Or maybe—and he inwardly shuddered—maybe she had received a blow to the head and been knocked out and was even then sinking slowly to the bottom.

Zach grew frantic. He turned right and left, seeking some sign. But the sunlight did not penetrate far enough. All was murk and shadow.

Where are you? Zach mentally screamed.

There!

A small figure floated barely a dozen feet away, head down, arms and legs dangling limply.

Zach's heart leaped into his throat. He flew to her, cleaving the water fit to rival a fish. Clamping an arm around her waist, he kicked upward. She did not stir or otherwise react. As they broke the surface, he clasped her to him and shook her. "Lou! Lou! Can you hear me?" She did not respond. Her eyes did not open. Chin slack on her chest, she was deathly pale.

"God, no!" Zach breathed.

Canoes materialized on each side. Nate reached down and took Lou. Swinging her up as if she weighed no more than a feather, he gently deposited her in the bottom of his canoe

In the other canoe, Winona and Blue Water Woman both offered their hands to Zach. "Climb in," his mother urged.

"I'll stay with Lou," Zach said.

Shakespeare glided up and leaned over to see Lou. "Is she breathing?"

Nate bent and put a hand over her mouth and nose. "I don't think so. I don't feel anything."

"*Lou!*" Zach cried, and started to scramble up, rocking his father's canoe.

"Hold off!" Shakespeare commanded. To Nate he said, "We must act quickly! Pick her up with her back to you and wrap your arms around her middle. Let the upper half of her body sag some."

Nate did not ask why. He did it.

"Now clench your hands together over her belly,"

Shakespeare said, "and pump your hands up under her ribs. Don't be timid, neither. You have to do it hard and fast."

Nate looked at him.

"I know," Shakespeare said.

"But what if—"

"Would you rather she were dead? Hurry, Horatio!"

Zach did not understand why his father hesitated. Lou had stopped breathing. They must not delay a single instant. "If you don't, I will," he said, and again began to climb in.

Nate did as McNair had instructed, pumping his arms in and out, gouging his knuckles deep. He did it half a dozen times, but he might as well have been squeezing a tree for all the good it did. Dread rising, he pumped harder and faster. He willed himself not to think of her possible condition and what this might do to her. In and out, in and out, he rammed his fists nearly to her spine.

"Please, Lou," Zach said. "Please."

Nate despaired of reviving her. On an impulse, he stood up, causing the canoe to wobble and tilt. He might have gone over the side had Zach not held on to the gunwale to steady it. Upright, he tried again. Lou was bent almost in half, her head hanging low.

Nate rammed his fists once, twice, a third time, and suddenly water gushed from Lou's mouth. She weakly stirred, and groaned. "It's working!" he cried, and in his excitement, rammed his fists into her harder than ever.

Something other than water spewed from Lou's open mouth and spattered the canoe. She coughed and wheezed and flailed, her eyes snapping open in alarm. "What? Where?"

"You are safe," Nate said, and eased her down as Zach swung a leg up and over and squatted on the other side of her, his arm around her shoulders.

"Lou? It's me, Zach. Are you all right?"

Unable to stop coughing, Lou wagged a hand at him and bent over again. Her shoulders shook and she moaned.

"Thanks, Pa," Zach said. "You saved her."

Nate did not reply. He was thinking of something else.

"Lou?" Zach tried again. "You nearly drowned. Pa had to almost break you in two to get you to breathe."

Gasping in breaths, Louisa said, "It feels like he did." But she raised her head and smiled at Nate. "Thank you. I thought I might be a goner when I went under."

Zach kissed her on the cheek and stroked her hair. "You had me worried for a bit there."

Lou stared at his dripping buckskins. "Was it you who jumped in and got me out?"

"I couldn't let you sink," Zach said. "You owe me a backrub."

Lou caressed his brow, then had to bend over again. The wet sounds gave way to dry, racking heaves. At length she subsided and swiped at her dripping mouth with a sleeve. "Lordy, if I had known this would happen, I wouldn't have eaten so much breakfast."

"We have to get you to shore, little lady," Shakespeare said.

Lou shook her head. "Don't be silly. I am fine. We have to keep after whatever did this to me."

"You're the one being silly," Zach said. "We are taking you home so you can rest, and that's all there is to it."

"Since when did you get so bossy?"

Winona was easing her canoe in closer. "I agree with my son," she said. "You need a hot bath, and then you should climb into bed and stay there until tomorrow morning."

"But it's not even noon yet!" Louisa objected. "I refuse to let you make a fuss over me."

"When you married my son you became my daughter, and my daughters always do as I say"

Their argument was interrupted by Wakumassee and Degamawaku, who had drifted in from the west. They commenced pointing excitedly, and yelling.

"Look! Look! There!"

The thing was coming back.

A Glimpse of Mystery

Shakespeare McNair refused to let anyone else be hurt. They were out on the lake at his bidding, their lives imperiled because of his belief the creature posed a threat. Louisa had very nearly drowned, and if the lake beast rammed another of their craft— Shakespeare was not about to let that happen. Suddenly pushing away from the others, he paddled his canoe into the path of the oncoming swell.

"What are you doing?" Nate demanded.

"Carcajou!" Blue Water Woman cried.

Shakespeare ignored them. He swung his canoe broadside to the swell and snatched up one of the harpoons. Rising, he balanced precariously on the balls of his feet and tensed for the throw.

Shakespeare had never been on a whaling vessel, but like most people, he was well aware of the particulars of the trade. The industry had existed since the late 1600s when Nantucket fishermen first began hunting whales for their livelihood. Half a century later, thanks to the valuable oil in their heads, sperm whales became the favorite catch.

Many a youth, inspired by dreams of an exciting

life at sea and the big money to be made, yearned to be a whaler. Shakespeare himself caught the whaling fever; for a while he had been torn between his hankering for a life at sea and his yearning to travel west of the Mississippi. As fate would have it, the mountains and the prairie won out over the oceans, but it was a close thing.

Now, with the hissing swell sweeping toward him, Shakespeare prepared to cast his harpoon as a whaler would. He sought in vain to see the animal he had come to slay, but all he could see was a dark shape.

"Carcajou!" Blue Water Woman screamed a second time.

Shakespeare cast the harpoon with all the power in his frame. He was old, but he was far from puny, and he had every hope that could he but pierce its head or body, he could put an end to the thing.

The harpoon flew true. It struck the swell right where Shakespeare wanted it to, at the point where the silhouette suggested the head should be. By rights, the tip should have sheared through the water and cleaved the beast underneath. But it was swept aside. Whether the rushing water deflected it or it glanced off the creature, Shakespeare couldn't say. He heard his wife shout something, and then the swell slammed into his canoe with the impact of a charging bull buffalo. Shakespeare felt the canoe rise up under him and tip. He threw himself out, or tried to, in an attempt to dive clear. Instead, jarring pain shot up both his legs, and the next thing he knew, he was under the water with a riot of frothing bubbles all around him.

And that was not all.

Shakespeare was aware of the canoe on its side above him, and of the gargantuan shape that had flipped it over. The thing had slowed and was turning.

It was coming back for him.

Levering his arms and legs, Shakespeare rose. He had to swim wide of the canoe, and he was still under the surface when his lower legs were struck a heavy blow. The forced knocked him back and down. Racked with pain, he glanced at his legs—and there it was.

The water devil, the creature, the *thing* was just below him. It was huge. He was willing to swear on a stack of Bibles that it was twenty feet long if it was an inch. Although his lungs were shrieking for air, Shakespeare did not rise. Not yet. Bending, he tried to pierce the gloom, made darker by the shadow of the canoe. Then a glimmer of sunlight penetrated, casting the thing's silhouette in relief against its watery domain.

It was a fish.

There could be no doubt. Shakespeare saw fins. Front fins and rear fins, a fin on top and possibly on the bottom toward the tail. The tail itself was split in the middle. The top half and the bottom half were not the same size, as in most fish. The top was twice as big and three times as long.

Shakespeare strained his eyes, but he could not tell what kind of fish it was. He started to rise, wondering if it would attack him, when suddenly the giant exploded into motion. But not toward him. It shot down into the depths. Living lightning, it was there one instant, gone the next. The last he saw of it was the sweep of its tail.

Too late, Shakespeare realized he had stayed under

too long. His lungs would not be denied. He willed his mouth to stay shut, but his lips parted of their own accord. Cold water gushed into his mouth and nose and down his throat. He gagged and sucked in more water. His movements became strangely sluggish. He could see the surface, so near and yet so far, but he could not reach it. His body would not respond as it should.

Darkness overcame him. Shakespeare's consciousness dimmed. He felt cold, clear to his marrow.

Then the darkness became total.

She went over the side before anyone could stop her.

They all saw the body, floating limp. Blue Water Woman cried out, "There he is!" and dived. She swam smoothly, despite her knee-length dress, and she had an arm around Shakespeare within seconds.

That was all it took for Nate to bring his canoe over. He grabbed hold of the back of Shakespeare's shirt and lifted. Zach and Lou moved to make room, but there was not enough and Nate had to lay Shakespeare's head and shoulders across Lou's legs.

"Is he—?" Blue Water Woman asked anxiously, treading water.

Nate saw his friend twitch. Putting a hand on Shakespeare's stomach, he pushed as hard as he could.

Water spewed from Shakespeare's mouth. Gasping and coughing, he opened his eyes and looked about him in confusion, then calmed.

"Oh, it's only you, Horatio. For a second there I thought I was being stomped by an angry elk."

Blue Water Woman clung to the side and peered over at her man. "Are you all right?"

Shakespeare looked toward her, and coughed. "You dived in to save me, didn't you?"

"It seemed like a good idea."

"Lordy. I will never hear the end of this one."

"No, you will not."

Shakespeare smiled and reached up, and their fingers brushed. "If I have not told you that I love you today, permit me to remedy my oversight."

"You nearly died."

"An exaggeration if ever I heard one." Shakespeare turned to Nate. "This is not going as well as we planned."

"We must get you to shore."

"I am fine."

"We must get *Lou* to shore," Nate amended.

Shakespeare blinked. "Oh. Yes, we must. I had forgotten." He slowly sat up and grinned at his wife. "Are you going to cling there all the way back?"

Winona had brought her canoe in and now offered her arm to Blue Water Woman. "Here, let me help you."

Presently, their stricken armada was underway.

"Wait!" Shakespeare exclaimed. "What about my canoe?"

Nate pointed.

Only one end was still above water, and it was filling fast. Trailing bubbles, the canoe slowly slipped from sight, leaving concentric ripples to mark the spot.

"There was a hole in it as big as a melon," Zach said.

"That makes two the fish sent to the bottom," Shakespeare said. "And after all the work we put into them."

"We should have made dugouts," Zach said. "That thing can't knock a hole in them."

"We aren't licked," Shakespeare said. "We will make more canoes and be back out here in no time." He looked at Nate, expecting him to say something. "Did you hear me, Horatio?"

"I heard."

"Fish got your tongue?"

"We will talk about it after we get you and Lou out of those wet clothes and in bed."

"Since when is a little wet worth so much fuss?" Shakespeare replied. "I am as well as I can be, I tell you."

"Take it up with your wife when we get back."

"You fight dirty." Shakespeare shifted and regarded Louisa. "How about you, young lady? You look pale."

"I am as fine as you, but my lunkhead of a husband still wants to put me to bed."

"I share your indignation. The way some people carry on about nearly drowning is ridiculous. But I agree with your husband on this."

Zach draped an arm around Lou's shoulders, and glared. "You and your stupid water devil."

"I beg your pardon?"

"I nearly lost her," Zach said. "And we would not have been out here but for you."

Shakespeare winced. "I grant you that. But your logic is faulty. If I were to suggest we go hunting, and while we were up in the mountains a Blackfoot put an arrow into your leg, would that be my fault?"

"Don't try to confuse me," Zach said.

"I will not accept blame that is not wholly mine. If your spleen is agitated, I suggest you direct it at the fish."

Nate glanced over his shoulder. "You keep calling it that. What makes you so sure?"

"I saw it, Horatio. As I am living and breathing again, I saw it. A fish such as mortal eyes have not beheld since the dawn of creation."

Zach snorted.

"He is not the flower of courtesy," Shakespeare quoted. "Scoff if you will, Zachary, but you saw the size of the thing even if you did not get a clear look at the thing itself."

"A fish," Nate repeated.

"You sound disappointed," Shakespeare said.

"I was half hoping it was something else," Nate said. "Something more." The legends of the water creatures, so common among so many tribes, had led him to think they would encounter the new and unknown.

"What more do you want?" Shakespeare asked. "A fish that size qualifies as a marvel."

Nate did not see how. Exceptionally large fish were often reported to inhabit lakes and rivers, to say nothing of the gigantic denizens of the seven seas. He mentioned as much.

"I grant you it is not as big as a whale," Shakespeare said. "And I seem to recollect hearing that some sharks grow over twenty feet long, and that there is a critter called a whale shark that grows to pretty near sixty. So maybe our monster is puny compared to them, but it is still a monster."

"It is a fish," Nate said, stroking his paddle. "You said so yourself."

"What difference does that make? It is a name, nothing more. That which we call a rose by any other word would—" Shakespeare stopped abruptly.

Waku had shouted and was jerking his arm. "Look! Look there! It come again!"

Not quite forty feet away was another swell. Their aquatic nemesis was pacing the canoes.

Lou gripped Zach's arm and swallowed. "What is that thing up to now?"

"Don't worry," Zach said, squeezing her. "It won't attack us again." But he did not feel as certain as he tried to sound.

"That blasted critter is taunting us," Shakespeare said. "The fiend is rubbing our noses in our defeat."

"It's a fish," Nate said again.

"Fish, smish. Have you not been baited by bears? And what about those wolverines that stalked us? Or that time you waged war against a demon of a mountain lion?"

"They were not fish."

Shakespeare let out an indignant harrumph. "Were I a finny dweller of the deep, I would take exception to your slander. To hear you talk, all fish are by nature dullards and do not share a whit of brain between them."

"They are fish."

"By God, say that one more time and I will scream!" Shakespeare declared. "Honestly, Horatio. I don't know what has gotten into you."

Nate twisted around and gave a pointed look at Louisa and then at McNair. "What was it you once said to me?" He paused. "Now I remember. A great deal of your wit lies in your sinews."

"Zounds," Shakespeare said. "Hoisted by my own petard. Does this mean you have changed your mind about smiting the brute?"

Nate resumed paddling and did not answer.

"Verily, this does not bode well."

Zach said, "I know *I* have changed my mind. All this over a *fish*? I don't care how big it is."

"And you don't care about what it did to your wife, either?" Shakespeare asked.

"Don't get me started again."

The swell continued to pace them until they drew near the west shore, close to Nate's cabin. When they were an arrow's flight out, with typical suddenness the swell shrank to nothing.

"Good riddance!" Lou exclaimed.

The canoes scraped bottom and they clambered out to drag them up onto land.

Shakespeare shook a fist at the lake, bellowing, "You have not seen the last of us, fish! We are in this to the death!" He smiled at the others. "Are you with me?"

No one answered.

Devious to The Bone

Shakespeare McNair took to lying in bed as eagerly as he would to lying on broken glass. He could not wait to get up and get on with his campaign against the lurker in the depths, but his wife insisted he rest while she went to make tea. He wanted coffee, but she said tea would be better for him.

"This is a fine state of affairs," Shakespeare groused to her departing back, "when a man my age is treated like a one-year-old."

From the doorway Blue Water Woman replied, "I would put—what do white women call them? Ah, yes. I would put diapers on you if we had any."

"I wouldst thou did itch from head to foot," Shakespeare quoted. "And I would not lift a finger to help you scratch." But his barb was wasted; he was alone. With a sigh of annoyance he clasped his hands behind his head and propped his head in his hands and his hands on the pillow.

Shakespeare felt terrible about the outcome of the day's effort: Louisa nearly drowned, him only slightly less waterlogged, and two canoes destroyed. "Not exactly a success," he said to the ceiling. He had planned so carefully, too. The extra canoes, the harpoons—they should have been enough, but they weren't. They should have done the job, but they didn't.

The fault did not lie with them. They had done all that was humanly possible. Their mistake, if it could be called that, was in going out to engage an enemy they knew nothing about. Ignorance had been the cause of their downfall. 'Know thy enemy' was coined for a reason.

What *did* they know? Shakespeare asked himself. What had they learned so far? He mentally ticked off the short list: they knew the creature was a fish, they knew harpoons were useless against it, and they knew it would fight, and fight fiercely, in defense of its domain.

"Not much, is it?" Shakespeare continued his conversation with the rafters. Certainly, none of their paltry knowledge would help him destroy the thing. Frowning, he closed his eyes and tried to relax, but he was asking the impossible of his racing mind.

"There has to be something," Shakespeare said. Again he went over his list: it was a fish, it had the temperament of a mad bull, it was more intelligent—in his opinion—than any fish he ever heard of, it liked to eat ducks, it stayed in the—

Shakespeare sat up. "It likes to eat ducks," he said out loud. Or was it, he mused, that the thing was partial to meat covered in feathers? He chuckled, an idea taking form. He was still contemplating when Blue Water Woman returned, bearing a tray with the cup of the tea she had promised, along with a steaming bowl of soup.

"What is this, wench? The condemned man is treated to a last meal?"

"What are you babbling about?

"Were I a building, I would be on the verge of ruin," Shakespeare said, moving his arms so she could set the tray in his lap.

"Does this have anything to do with your silly notion that you are being treated like a child?"

Shakespeare tugged at his white mane. "You don't see infants with a mop of snow."

"We are back to that again."

"To what?"

"Never mind." Blue Water Woman tapped the saucer. "I put toza in the tea."

Shakespeare did not need to ask why. He was familiar with dozens of Indian remedies, everything from bitterroot for sore throats to juniper berries for bladder problems to the root of the horse-tail plant for sores. Toza was a tonic for those who were run down.

"Drink it."

"Well moused, lion," Shakespeare quoted. But he obliged her and took several sips. Setting the cup down, he picked up the spoon and was about to dip it into the soup when the aroma tingled his nose. "Unless my nostrils are mistaken, this is chicken soup."

"We were out of badger meat," Blue Water Woman bantered. They hardly ever ate badger.

"A fowl by any other feather," Shakespeare said, and cackled. He eagerly spooned some of the broth into his mouth and delightedly smacked his lips. "Yes, indeed. It will do, and do nicely."

"I am glad you like my soup."

"I like your feathers more, madam," Shakespeare said. "How many would you say we have, give or take an egg?"

Blue Water Woman could not hide her puzzlement.

"What are you on about? I do not have feathers. As for eggs, I collected eleven from the coop this morning."

"Eleven eggs but no feathers."

"Will you stop with the feathers? You are making less sense than usual, which I did not think was possible."

"On the contrary, my dear," Shakespeare gloated. "You have given me a most wonderful inspiration."

"In regards to what?"

Shakespeare spooned more soup into his mouth. "Between the feathers and the tea, my vigor and vim have been restored. I am ready to slay that finny dragon."

"No."

"Excuse me?"

"I talked it over with Winona on our way to shore, and she agrees it is entirely too dangerous. We should let the water devil or fish or whatever it is be. Let it get on with its life and we will get on with ours."

"You would give up just like that?" Shakespeare said, and snapped his fingers.

"You could have been killed. Lou nearly died. What more will it take to convince you to leave well enough alone?"

"Have I mentioned lately how wonderful your English is? If you were behind a screen, and I did not know you were a Flathead, I would swear you were white."

"Are you trying to change the subject?"

"Me?" Shakespeare touched his chest in mock amazement. "Do you honestly think I would stoop so low?"

"Lower, if you thought you could get away with it."

"Is't come to this? In faith, hath the world not one man but he will wear his cap with suspicion?"

"I know how your mind works," Blue Water Woman said. "You are as devious a man as any who ever lived, red or white."

"I thank you."

"It was not a compliment, husband. You are up to something. Confess what it is and I will not be nearly as mad as when I find out on my own."

Shakespeare covered her hand with his and gazed up into her eyes. "Since brevity is the soul of wit, and tediousness the limbs and outward flourishes, I will be brief," he quoted. "I have no idea what you are talking about."

"Don't you?" Blue Water Woman said. "Whatever you are plotting, do not do it. I ask you this as your wife of many winters."

"I live to please you," Shakespeare said.

"Good."

"But I am also a man."

"Not so good." Blue Water Woman placed her other hand on his shoulder and leaned down. "Let it go. Let it go. Let it go."

"You are a most marvelous parrot."

"I mean it."

"I am yours to command."

"You mean that?"

"I am a living fount of truth," Shakespeare said. "You can trust me to do what I have to."

"Very well." Blue Water Woman smiled and straightened. "I have chores to do. Eat, then rest. By tomorrow you should be back to your old self."

"Assuredly," Shakespeare said. He waited until she had left the bedroom, then snickered and said to himself, "A fox has nothing on me." He ate heartily, plotting as he chewed and swallowed, and washed the chicken soup down with the tea.

Content with the food and his plot, and feeling as warmly snug as a bear in its den, Shakespeare pulled the blankets up. He needed to get as much rest as he could. He let himself drift off, and to his surprise, he slept so long that when he woke up the bedroom was dark and the front room was lit by the glow of their lamp. Yawning and stretching, he sat up. He was about to slide out of bed when he remembered his brainstorm. Grinning slyly, he called out to his wife and erased the grin before she appeared.

"You are finally up."

"Don't blame me. It was your idea," Shakespeare said grumpily.

"I am glad you slept so long. You needed the rest." Blue Water Woman came over and pressed a palm to his forehead. "You do not have a fever. How do you feel?"

"Still a little tired," Shakespeare fibbed. "But hungry enough to eat an entire buffalo, hooves and horns included."

"You stay right there. I will bring your supper to you." Blue Water Woman kissed him on the cheek. "I am happy you have decided to listen to reason."

Shakespeare watched her go out, marveling at how little she truly knew him after all their years together. Never in his entire life had he ever given up on anything. He was not about to give up on this.

The tantalizing aroma of cooking food filled the cabin. Shakespeare's stomach rumbled. He was famished. When she brought in a tray with a sizzling slab of venison, hot potatoes smothered in gravy, and green beans, he ate with relish, savoring every bite. The deer meat, in particular, was delicious. It had been a staple of his diet for so long, he preferred it over beef. Three cups of piping hot coffee helped fill his belly. As he was pouring his last cup, Blue Water Woman came in and sat on the edge of the bed.

"I have something to ask you."

"Ask away," Shakespeare warily said, afraid she had guessed what he intended to do and would insist he not do it.

"That talk we had a while back about each of our families getting a cow," Blue Water Woman said. "Do you still want one?"

Shakespeare smiled in relief. "I do if you do."

"I talked about it out on the lake with Winona. It was Nate's idea, and it is a good one. We will have milk every day, and I can churn butter. I have never done that, but if white women can do it, I can, too."

"A cow it is," Shakespeare said. "Nate and I aim to ride to Bent's Fort in a couple of weeks to see about buying some from any pilgrims who might be bound for Oregon Country." Invariably, in every wagon train, more than a few emigrants had cows tied to the back of their wagons, or else the cows were bunched in a common herd.

Blue Water Woman caressed his cheek. "You are a good husband. Have I told you that of late?"

"Not often enough." Shakespeare hid his shame by swallowing more coffee.

"You can get out of bed if you want and come out to your rocking chair and read the Bard."

"I think I will sleep a bit more," Shakespeare said. "I am still a mite drowsy. Must be that tasty feed of yours." He did not mention that he needed to rest now so he could be up later.

"As you wish." Blue Water Woman kissed him, took the tray, and padded from the bedroom.

Shakespeare felt bad about deceiving her. He was not one of those men who played false with their women just to get their way. "But I have it to do," he said out loud.

As if anticipating the trial he intended to put it to, his body did not object when he tried to go back to sleep. He did not fidget and toss and turn, as he was sometimes wont to do, but succumbed to slumber within a few minutes and slept the sleep of the innocent, although he was anything but. When next he awoke, Blue Water Woman informed him it was almost nine o'clock.

Shakespeare got up and went outside. When he came back in, he did as she had suggested and sat in the rocking chair by the fireplace and opened his well-used leather-bound volume of the works of the wordsmith he most admired. But for once he had no interest in reading the plays and sonnets. He could not stop thinking about his next attempt to put an end to the fish.

That was how he thought of it now, as *the fish*. He had seen it with his own eyes, and it had nearly drowned him. If ever combat was personal, this was. The fish had thrown down the gauntlet and Shakespeare had accepted. It was the fish or him, and it would not be him.

His conscience pricked him anew when they turned in for the night. He snuggled up to Blue Water Woman and nuzzled her neck with his beard, giving her the kind of kiss he usually reserved for nights when they planned to be frisky. Planned, because Blue Water Woman insisted on knowing in advance, a quirk of hers he never fully grasped. He liked to be spontaneous; she liked to plan everything out. Even *that*.

Inadvertently, Blue Water Woman added salt to his wound by saying dreamily as she drifted off, "Thank you for listening to me. I meant what I said about you being a good husband."

"Tell me that again in the morning," Shakespeare said.

He tried to get a little more sleep but couldn't. By the clock on the small table, it was a little past midnight when he eased back the covers and swung his feet to the floor. He dressed in near silence, thankful, for once, that she liked to sleep with a candle burning. Another of her quirks. The only thing that stopped him from complaining about it was the he had more quirks than she did.

Shakespeare had a lot to gather. Ammo pouch, powder horn, possibles bag, pistols, rifle, knife, a parfleche with food, the coil of rope that hung on a peg, their lantern, and perhaps the most important item of all, the small grappling iron he had for when he went after mountain sheep. The Big Horns lived up in the rocky heights at the highest altitudes. To get to them entailed a lot of climbing, and the iron always came in handy.

Shakespeare was careful not to let the door creak as he slipped out into the cool of night. Hurrying around to the corral, he lit the lantern and saddled his white mare. Next he went to the chicken coop. Several hens clucked and fluttered, but they were used to him, and when he spoke softly, they quieted.

Regretfully, he picked up the one he had decided to take, the smallest of the hens, and carried her out. Then came the hard part.

Shakespeare carried the limp body to the mare and tied it to his saddle. He led the mare a short way from the cabin, climbed on, and glanced at the lake.

"I am coming for you."

The Best Laid Brainstorms

The canoes were where they had left them.

Shakespeare tied the mare to Nate's corral and carried everything he was taking to the Nansusequa dugout. The paddles and harpoons and net still lay on the bottom. He placed his rifle beside them. The rope, grappling iron, and dead chicken went in the bow. The parfleche with the food, in the stern. The lantern was last.

Shakespeare pushed the canoe out into the water and climbed in. He picked up one of the paddles and peered into the veil of darkness. The risk he was about to take gave him pause. But only for a few seconds. Squaring his shoulders, he commenced paddling.

At night the lake was deathly still. The ducks, the geese, the teal, all were silent. Were it not for the occasional splash of a fish, a person would never guess that the lake teemed with life during the day.

A brisk gust of wind sent goose bumps parading up and down his spine. He blamed it on the chill and suppressed a shudder.

The glow cast by his lantern illuminated a ten-foot circle. Beyond the light, all was liquid ink. He considered turning back and waiting until daylight. But if he did that, the others were bound to try and stop him. With any luck, he could do what he had to do and be back in his cabin by dawn.

It all depended on the fish. The thing had shown a fondness for waterfowl, so maybe fowl of another kind would appeal to its piscine taste buds.

The shore gradually receded. Shakespeare was alone with the canoe and the water and the dweller in the depths. He hoped that if the fish was going to attack, it would at least hold off until he was ready.

His plan was to paddle out to where he had seen the two birds taken. But in the dark, in open water, there were no landmarks, no means to tell where he was, other than the stars. He could approximate, but that was all.

The slight *splish* each time Shakespeare stroked the paddle, the swish of the canoe as it cleaved the surface, and the occasional splash of a fish were the only sounds. He listened for the howl of a wolf or the yip of a coyote, but the valley was as quiet as the lake.

Shakespeare hoped he was not wasting his time. He would never hear the end of the teasing if he spent all night on the lake and had nothing to show for it. He continued paddling until, as best as he could tell, he was about where the fish had taken the duck and the teal. Resting the paddle across the gunwales, he strained his senses for some sign of his quarry.

All was peaceful.

Working quickly, Shakespeare tied one end of the rope to the grappling iron. The rest of the rope he coiled in front of him.

The next step proved harder than he thought it would. The grappling iron had four hooks, or flukes.

They were sharp enough that he figured it would be easy to impale the chicken. But when he tried, he could not get the rounded ends to penetrate deep enough to hold fast.

"I do not need this nuisance," Shakespeare said. Drawing his knife, he made two deep cuts in the chicken, aligned the cuts with two of the hooks, and jammed the chicken onto the grappling iron. A few tugs satisfied him that the chicken would not slip off.

Lowering his improvised hook and bait over the side, Shakespeare fed out the rope until only a few feet remained. He needed to anchor it, but had nothing to tie it to. He briefly considered tying it to his leg, but the mental image of being yanked over the side persuaded him not to. The only other thing he could think of to tie it to was the spare paddle, which he wedged under him.

Years ago Shakespeare had heard that fish could sense prey from a long way off. The wriggle of a worm, the flutter of an insect's wings, were enough to bring a hungry fish streaking in for the kill. He began wriggling the rope in the hope it would have the same effect on *the* fish.

Another gust of wind provoked a shiver. Shakespeare stared to the west. The gusts were stronger than usual. He wondered if a front was moving in. The last thing he needed was to be caught on the lake in a thunderstorm. Sometimes the waves rose two and three feet high. He debated going back, but decided if a storm did break, he would have enough advance warning to reach shore.

Shakespeare continued to wriggle the rope. The quiet of the night and the near total dark gnawed on his nerves. It occurred to him that the fish could be lurking outside the ring of light and he would not know it. He reached for the lantern to extinguish it, then changed his mind. Without the light he could not see the rope, and he must be ready when the fish took the bait.

Shakespeare's uneasy feeling grew. He and the canoe were an island of light in an ocean of dark. The glow could be seen for miles. Possibly even from the bottom of the lake.

None of them knew how deep the lake was. Once, shortly after they built their cabins, Shakespeare and Nate had lashed together the logs they had left over and ventured out on the lake on the raft. Nate had the notion to find out how deep the lake was by tying a rock to a hundred-foot rope and lowering the rope until it struck bottom.

It didn't.

They added fifty feet, then fifty more, and when that was still not enough, Nate went to Bent's Fort for the express purpose of buying a hundred more. Surely, they had reasoned, three hundred feet would suffice.

It didn't.

The lake was more than three hundred feet deep. Shakespeare did not know how that compared to other mountain lakes, but three hundred feet was damn deep, deeper than most fish ever went. The thing he was up against was extraordinary if, in fact, it normally dwelled at the bottom.

To the best of Shakespeare's logic, there were three possibilities. Either the fish was an oversized member of a known species, it was of a species yet to be officially discovered, or it was a holdover from an earlier era, a relict from the time when, according to many Indians, the land and the water were overrun by huge animals of all kinds.

Shakespeare could not say what the fish was, but he hoped to have an answer by the rising of the sun.

Time passed. The swaying of the canoe lulled Shakespeare into lowering his chin to his chest and closing his eyes. He had no intention of drifting off, but before he could stop himself, he did.

Suddenly Shakespeare's head snapped up and his eyes opened. He tried to figure out what had woken him. The lake was as still and dark as it had been before, save for the splash of a fish.

Shakespeare started to succumb to drowsiness again. Another splash, louder than the first, brought him out of it. Acting on the assumption that the bigger the fish, the bigger the splash, he gazed about for the source.

The rope had not moved. The chicken still dangled in the depths. Leaning back, Shakespeare sighed. He had forgotten how much waiting there was with fishing, whether the fisherman was after bass or sunfish or catfish—or monster fish.

Shakespeare wondered if the monster might not be a catfish. They sometimes grew to exceptional lengths. He was not sure exactly how big they could get, but he seemed to recollect hearing that twelve feet was not out of the question.

The dugout swayed slightly.

Stiffening, Shakespeare raised the lantern. The wind was not strong enough to account for the movement. He peered over the side, but it was like gazing into a black well. "Was it you?" he asked the water.

As if in answer, the dugout abruptly rose half an inch, then settled back down again. In reflex, Shakespeare grabbed the gunwales. He waited for another bump or the rising of a swell, but nothing happened.

Not so much as a twitch from the rope.

Shakespeare picked up a harpoon, then put it down again. The cocoon of water the fish displaced when it moved at high speed had deflected Zach's cast. What made him think he would fare any better? He drew a pistol instead.

The lake was still again. Above him a multitude of stars sparkled. More wind renewed his concern about an incoming front. Once again he debated heading for shore and safety.

Then the rope moved. Not much, no more than a shake, but something was interested in the bait.

Scarcely breathing, Shakespeare glued his eyes to it. It moved again and his heart jumped. It occurred to him that maybe a smaller fish was nipping at the chicken, and his elation vanished. It surged again when he realized a small fish could not move the rope like that. It would take a fish of considerable size. It would take *his* fish.

Shakespeare smiled at this thought. *His* fish? It was not a pet. It was his adversary, his enemy, his personal dragon.

Another jerk on the rope prompted Shakespeare to lightly wrap his hand around it. He felt an ever-so-slight vibration. "What are you doing, fish?" he wondered.

The vibration stopped.

Once more Shakespeare waited with bated breath, but the rope stayed still. He feared the fish had lost interest, that a chicken was no substitute for a duck.

That was when the rope jumped taut. Shakespeare started to whoop in triumph, but the shout died in his throat as the paddle he had tied the end of the rope to started to slide out from under him. Setting down his pistol, he gripped the paddle with both hands and shifted so all his weight was on it. It worked. The paddle stopped moving.

The canoe moved instead.

The rope began cleaving the water, pulling the canoe after it. Shakespeare chuckled, pleased that his ploy had worked. The fish had taken the bait and swallowed the chicken. Now it was only a matter of time before the fish tired and he could haul it up out of the benighted depths and dispatch it.

The canoe was gaining speed. Apparently the dugout was no more of a hindrance to the fish than a leaf would be.

Shakespeare tugged on the rope, but he could not draw it up. The fish was too strong or too heavy, or both.

The canoe went faster, knifing the water more swiftly than Shakespeare could ever hope to paddle. More swiftly, even, than two men could. The sheer brute strength the fish possessed was a wonderment.

A sliver of doubt pricked Shakespeare, but he cast it aside. His plan would work. It might take longer to tire the fish, was all.

The bow began rising and falling, rising and falling, slapping down with enough force to rattle Shakespeare's teeth and spray water all over him. He hunched his shoulders, determined to ride it out.

Suddenly the rope changed direction. Shakespeare clung on, his hair and shirt soaked. Cold drops trickled down his chest and back, raising yet more goose flesh. "Damn you, fish," he growled. He had not counted on anything like this. He had not counted on anything like this at all.

Incredibly, the dugout went faster. The bow was smacking the surface in violent cadence, the harpoons and his rifle and pistol clattering and bouncing madly about. He worried the Hawken would go over the side. He could always get another rifle, but it would mean riding all the way to St. Louis, and Lord, he did not want to do that.

The rope was a rigid bar. Try as he might, Shakespeare could not budge it. He was at the mercy of the fish. His wife's warnings came back to him, and he was almost sorry he had not heeded her. Almost.

To complicate matters, either the canoe was moving so fast it was whipping his beard and hair, or the wind from the west was gusting relentlessly, which did not bode well.

"Damn," Shakespeare said again. Too many things were going wrong. In frustration he wrenched on the rope, but all he succeeded in doing was to give his palms rope burn.

The lantern tilted. Another hard jostle and it would fall.

Shakespeare had forgotten about it. He would be in total darkness if it went out, an unappealing prospect. Lunging, he set it back up and slid it flush against the inner curve of the bow so it would not tip.

A loud hissing arose. Shakespeare marveled anew at the prodigious might the fish displayed.

Again the dugout changed direction. By now Shakespeare had lost all sense of where he was. He might be out in the middle, he might be close to shore. All he could say for certain was that he did not like the predicament his stubbornness had placed him in.

The canoe smacked down so hard, Shakespeare nearly tumbled. He had to grip the sides to stay on his knees. The next instant the whole canoe commenced shimmying, shaking him to his marrow.

Shakespeare had a terrible thought: What if the

canoe collided with something? Drifting logs were not uncommon. Deer and elk sometimes went for a swim. Once, years ago, he had caught sight of a black bear splashing about.

Once more the dugout changed direction. Seconds later, yet again. A few more seconds, and a third time. It suggested the fish was growing frantic.

Shakespeare took that as a good sign and clung on. He wished he knew where he was. He sought a glimpse of a cabin but could not even see the shore. The bow abruptly dipped, almost spilling him, but the dugout righted itself and he was safe.

Safe, Shakespeare somberly reflected. The notion was laughable. He was anything but.

The bow slid under the surface and went on sinking. With a start, Shakespeare realized the fish might pull the dugout under. He had one recourse: he must cut the rope. His hand flew to the sheath at his hip and he started to draw his knife. But his fingers had barely gripped the hilt when the canoe gave the most violent lurch yet. He was propelled forward. Flinging out his arms, he kept from smashing into the lantern, but his forehead hit the side. It was like being kicked by a mule.

Pain exploded, Shakespeare's vision spun, and his gut was wrenched by invisible fingers. He struggled to sit up, but his body would not do as he wanted. "No!" he cried, and got his hands under him.

Inner blackness swallowed all there was left to swallow.

Ordeal

Shakespeare McNair opened his eyes and thought he was dead. He was floating in a misty cloud. Pale grayish wisps hung in the air in front of him, writhing like ethereal serpents. He reached up to touch one and it dissolved at his touch.

The mist was everywhere; above him, below him, around him, a vaporous cocoon his vision could not penetrate.

Shakespeare had never been sure how the afterlife would be, but he'd never imagined it would be like this. A lot of folks were certain they knew: heaven would have pearly gates and great white mansions and winged angels singing in celestial choirs; hell would be fire and brimstone and unending torment. It was Shakespeare's view that it was presumptuous to anticipate the Almighty; he would find out when he got there. Wherever *there* turned out to be.

Then pain racked his head, and when he gave a start, his elbow bumped wood. In the distance a gull shrieked.

Shakespeare came back to his senses. He was not floating in a cloud; he was floating in the dugout. He had not died; he had been knocked unconscious. The mist was not heavenly vapor; it was fog.

Disgusted with himself, Shakespeare sat up. He was surprised to see that the lantern had gone out. It had enough fuel to burns for hours. He glanced skyward but could not see for the fog. But judging by the raucous shrieks of the gulls and the quacks of ducks and cries of other fowl, the new day had dawned. He had been out all night.

Shakespeare went to turn and the pain grew worse. Gringerly, he touched his brow. He had a nasty gash and was caked with dried blood. "This is a piece of malice," he quoted to the wispy tendrils.

McNair took stock. The dugout was intact and afloat, the paddles and harpoons and his rifle and parfleche were still lying on the bottom. Other than the gash, he was fine. There was no reason to head for shore.

Leaning over the side, Shakespeare dipped his hand in the water and splashed some on his face and neck. As cold as ice, it helped revitalize him. He picked up the pistol he had dropped and tucked the flintlock under his wide leather belt.

The rope lay limp next to him. Either it had snapped or the fish had come loose of the grappling iron and gone on its way.

"If I did not have bad luck, I would not have any luck at all," Shakespeare groused. He gripped the rope to pull it up and suddenly it came alive in his hands. Instantly the canoe leaped forward, and the paddle he had tied the rope to started to rise. Lunging, he got his legs on top of it and bore down with all his weight.

The canoe moved faster.

Shakespeare bent over the side to peer into the water, but he could not see for the fog. A hiss fell on his ears.

"You blunt monster, with uncounted heads," Shakespeare quoted. "All the whole heap must die."

As last night, so now: the dugout bounced violently, the bow rising and falling as if it were a flat stone skimming the surface. The fish must not be swimming in a straight line but in an undulating fashion, rising up and going down, over and over. Why it would do that was beyond him. But it vindicated his decision to use the dugout and not a bark canoe. By now, the bark craft would have been shattered to bits and pieces.

Shakespeare put his hand on the bundled net. His plan still might succeed. Tire the fish, draw it to the surface, and slay it with a harpoon, either outright, or if he could not get a good cast, then get the net over it and pull it close enough to thrust a harpoon clean through the beast. "Malignant thing!" he quoted. "By my hand, I'll turn my mercy out of doors, and make a stock fish of thee!"

The canoe gave a wild lurch as it changed direction. Shakespeare grabbed the side. He winced as the paddle nearly came out from under him, smacking his shin hard.

Shakespeare wished he could tell where they were. They might be close to land, and a shout would bring his wife and friends to his aid. But no. He refused to call for help. He'd gotten himself into this predicament; he would prevail without imposing on them. Yes, he was being stubborn. He was succumbing to the sin of pride. But he could not help it. He was acting on his belief that it was in their best interest to dispose of the thing before it disposed of one of them.

The rope abruptly went slack and the dugout

coasted to a stop. Shakespeare peered over the side again, but he might as well try to see through mud. The damnable fog foiled him. He was tempted to tug on the rope, but didn't. It might provoke the fish into another mad run.

The minutes dragged. The fish was content to remain still. Shakespeare splashed more water on his head, which had taken to throbbing, then opened his parfleche and took out a bundle of pemmican Blue Water Woman had made. A mix of finely ground deer meat, fat, and chokecherries, it was just about his favorite food in all the world. He munched and mulled over his dilemma. Or should he say, the *fish's* dilemma. He had caught it. It could not shake loose the grappling iron. Eventually it would tire and be at his mercy. All he had to do was wait.

But for all his years, Shakespeare had never been the most patient of men. He could not stand to sit still when he could be doing something. In this instance, as soon as he finished another piece of pemmican, he made sure the parfelche was snug in the stern, then wrapped his hands around the rope and pulled. He wanted to provoke it. He wanted another underwater sprint and more after that, to exhaust the fish that much sooner.

But nothing happened. The rope did not snap rigid. The dugout did not move.

Shakespeare tugged harder. His first thought was that the fish had slipped free, but no, if that were the case, the rope would be slack. The fish was still caught. It must be resting.

"I have you, but you do not know it." Shakespeare smiled. By the end of the day he would have a surprise for his doubting Thomas of a wife and his best friend. The canoe shook, but not from the fish. The wind was stirring the lake and creating small waves.

Shakespeare had hoped the fog would soon disperse, but if anything it became thicker. What pale light there was began to fade, which told him the sun was being blotted out by clouds.

It could be that the storm he had been expecting was about to break.

The dugout had withstood battering by the beast, but battering by a tempest would be more than it could endure. It would be swamped and capsize, leaving Shakespeare at the pitiless mercy of the elements.

He had a decision to make. He could stay and continue his battle with the fish, or he could cut the rope and make for land, and safety. Craning his neck, he probed the fog above, seeking a break, looking for sign of thunderheads. But all he saw was fog.

Shakespeare shook his head. He had seen it through this far. He would stay and hope he was wrong about the storm.

A faint shout reached him. It sounded like someone calling his name. He did not answer. It was inevitable they would search for him, but he was determined to go it alone. Bad enough he had nearly cost Lou her life. He would not endanger anyone else.

The rope twitched.

Shakespeare braced himself, and it was well he did. The rope tightened and the dugout flew forward. Shakespeare hoped it was a dying spurt of energy. Sometimes, at the very last, animals marshaled their strength for a final effort. If not, if the creature's vitality was undiminished, he was no better off than when he first hooked the thing, which did not bode well for the outcome.

He kept watch for logs, but the fog was so thick he would not see one until he smashed into it. Then something appeared ahead of them. Something low in the water. Shakespeare braced for the worst. There was a thump and a crunch and a squawk that might have come from a goose. He looked back and thought he glimpsed the stricken bird flapping about.

Another thump and another crunch, and this time Shakespeare saw a dead goose pass under the bow. The dugout was plowing through a flock. "Get out of the way!" he shouted. "Take to the air!" Another crunch and another goose flapped and thrashed.

Suddenly the craft gave one of its violent lurches and was off in a whole new direction.

Shakespeare had given up trying to figure out where on the lake he was. To try was pointless until the fog dissipated.

With surprising abruptness, the fish stopped. The dugout was brought to a halt by the rope.

Now what? Shakespeare wondered. He waited a bit, then opened the parfleche and treated himself to another piece of pemmican.

The fog was growing darker. A new gust brought the scent of water, but that could just be the scent of the lake. Wishful thinking, it turned out.

Off in the distance thunder boomed.

Shakespeare swore. A storm was bad enough; a thunderstorm was a calamity. The deluge would fill the dugout, and he had nothing to bail with other than his hands.

As if the fish had heard, or maybe it was coincidence, the rope snapped taut and the dugout burst into motion. But it did not hurtle forward. The bow dipped and the stern rose off the water and Shakespeare had to grab the sides or be thrown out.

The fish was trying to dive! It wanted to go deeper and was trying to pull the canoe down after it. For a few uneasy moments Shakespeare imagined it succeeding, imagined being pitched into the water as the canoe vanished under the surface.

"No, by God!" Shakespeare clawed for his knife. He must cut the rope whether he wanted to or not. He bent, the blade inches from the hemp, when the rope went slack and the stern smacked down. Shakespeare landed hard on the paddles and harpoons, and agony coursed up his spine. Grunting, he tried to sit up just as the canoe surged forward.

Shakespeare was thrown against the side. He grunted again at a prick in his ribs. The prick was replaced by sharp pain, and looking down, he saw why. *He had stabbed himself.* Not deeply, but deep enough to draw blood.

Shakespeare indulged in more curses. He yanked the knife out and more blood flowed. "Damn me for a fool." Pressing his hand to the wound, he stanched the flow. But the dark stain on his shirt was not encouraging.

"Of all the stupid—" Shakespeare began. Another boom of thunder, closer than before, reminded him the rope still had to be cut. He pushed up onto his knees. Bracing himself, he slashed at it, but the dugout bounced and his stroke missed.

Wind buffeted his buckskins, a prelude to the riotous weather to come. He raised the knife again.

With a banshee shriek, the storm broke. Sheets of

driving rain pummeled him. It was like having a bottomless bucket of water thrown in his face. He blinked to clear his vision but could not see the end of his arm. Again he bent toward the rope, but a blast of wind slammed into him, stripping his breath and plastering his soaked buckskins to his body. A cold wind stung his skin and brought shivers.

Everything had gone to hell. Shakespeare's sole desire now was to survive. He groped for the rope and was thrown against the side when the canoe spun like a child's top. The fish was swimming in small circles. Shakespeare clung to the gunwale as nausea flooded through him, either from the spinning, or his wound, or both.

Water spilled in over the side. The waves were rising. Normally so serene, the lake was being churned into a maelstrom.

Between the wind and the rain, Shakespeare could scarely breathe. Gasping for air, he dropped onto his belly and felt about. He found the rope. This time nothing would stop him. But as he brought the knife up, the rope went slack and the spinning slowed.

A clap of thunder made his ears ring.

Shakespeare pulled on the rope and it stayed slack. Maybe the fish at long last had pulled loose.

The wind nearly snapped his head back. He looked up just as lightning rent the heavens and lit the sky. The fog was almost gone, whipped away by the fury of the tempest.

Shakespeare's heart sank.

The lake itself had been transformed into a monster. The water writhed and surged as if alive. White caps peaked the waves much as snow peaked the mountains, only these mountains were moving. As he looked on, a wave heaved up into a watery fist and smashed down over the dugout, knocking him flat.

Shakespeare had run out of time. He gripped the slack rope in his free hand and held it so he could cut it. A premonition made him look up just as another wave came crashing over the gunwale. Again he was knocked flat. The canoe tilted and settled back, water covering the bottom.

Shakespeare got to his knees, puzzled by a strange tightness around his left forearm. He tried to move his arm but couldn't. A flash of lightning revealed why. Somehow the slack rope had looped around his wrist. He twisted his arm, but the rope would not slide off. He tugged, but that only made the rope tighten.

"Damn it." Shakespeare let go of his knife and grabbed the rope to unwind it. Without any warning the rope went rigid, as it always did when the fish was about to move again. "No!" he shouted.

Jerked off balance, Shakespeare slammed down hard. His wrist, his whole arm, felt fit to be torn off. He gritted his teeth against the pain. The canoe was picking up speed, and the faster it went, the more pain he felt.

This was bad. This was very bad. Shakespeare tried to get to his knees but was yanked down. The rope was digging so deep into his flesh, his fingers were going numb.

Shakespeare rolled onto his side to try to get some slack in the rope. He did, for all of two seconds. He pried at it with his other hand but could not free his wrist.

The dugout hurtled headlong through the storm-tossed waters as lightning crackled and thunder crashed. Shakespeare managed to get to one knee and saw the knife at his feet. He reached for it just as the largest wave yet reared up out of the lake and curled above his head.

Tempest Fury

A ton of water smashed down. Shakespeare's temple struck the bottom of the dugout, and for a few harrowing instants he feared he would pass out again. A black veil nipped at him, and his stomach tried to climb up out of his throat. Only by force of will was he able to stay conscious and shove his stomach back down where it belonged.

His wrist was in torment. The rope was a vise, the other end lost in the darkling realm under the canoe. He groped for his knife, but it was not where he had seen it last. Frantic, he cast about, but it was not to be found. Washed over the side, most likely.

Then Shakespeare remembered the harpoons. Grabbing one a few inches below the tip, he commenced sawing at the rope. The tip was not as sharp as his knife, but it would suffice.

The canoe kept swaying and bouncing, and he was handicapped by having to use one hand.

Wet drops spattered him, multiplying rapidly. Another cannonade of thunder heralded the unleashing of the deluge in all its elemental fury.

Shakespeare focused on the rope and only the rope. The fish had slowed, but that might be temporary, and it was entirely possible that its next burst of speed might yank him clear out of the canoe or tear his arm clean off.

With the storm roaring around him, Shakespeare sliced at strand after strand. Time seemed to slow. A result of the knock on the head, he reckoned. Or was there more to it? Shakespeare would be the first to admit that he was not getting any younger. He liked to joke about his creaking joints and aching muscles, but the truth was, they *did* creak and ache. Remarkable though his stamina and strength were for his age, he was not the man he used to be. The thought broke his concentration. He had never truly regarded himself as *old* before, but maybe it was time he started. He had limits, and the smart thing to do was to respect those limits and not go traipsing out on a lake after a creature more formidable, in its way, than a grizzly or a buffalo.

Shakespeare resumed slicing. He had lost all feeling from his fingertips to his wrist, and now the numbness was spreading higher. He prayed to God he would not lose the hand. "I have grown rather attached to it," he said, and chuckled at his warped humor.

Shakespeare sliced as fast as he could, given how awkward it was to handle the harpoon with one hand. The canoe rocked without cease, threatening to upend him. *Do it, damn you!* he mentally shouted. *So what if you are old? Think of your wife and think of your friends and do it!*

As if in answer, the rope severed, and the end that trailed over the gunwale went sliding over the edge and was gone.

Wincing at the agony, Shakespeare unwound the

loop from his wrist. He wriggled his fingers, or tried to, to help restore his circulation, which only made the pain worse.

Unexpectedly, the canoe pitched, throwing him onto his good arm. Thinking the fish might be to blame, Shakespeare looked up—and gaped in astonishment.

The world had gone mad. Writhing black clouds filled the sky from horizon to horizon, broken by vivid jagged bolts. The rumble and boom of thunder was continuous. One bolt, quite near, sizzled the air with a sound like that of frying bacon and struck something on the lake in a brilliant flash. The rain was Noah's flood all over again. But the wind was the worst; it howled and screeched and churned the water into convulsions. It was the wind that gave birth to increasingly larger waves. The lake, once so tranquil, was in upheaval.

A wave caught the dugout and lifted it into the air, only to bring it smashing down with a jolt that jarred Shakespeare to his marrow. He had never seen the lake like this. It was just his luck—or lack of it—that he should be out in the canoe when the storm of the century swept in.

The fish was of no consequence now. All that mattered was surviving, staying alive so he could hold Blue Water Woman in his arms once again. So what if she would tease him with an endless litany of "I told you so"? She had been right and he had been wrong, and he was man enough to admit it.

Special moments rose unbidden in his memory. The first time he set eyes on her and was dazzled by her beauty; the deep, special love that blossomed; the giddy delight of taking her into his arms, and their first kiss. Lord, how he adored that woman! To think that he might lose her, or she him, because he had been too pigheaded to listen!

Another wave raised the dugout. Shakespeare braced himself as one side dipped lower than the other, using his good hand and his knees to keep from being catapulted out. He succeeded, but at the height of the wave, when he did not dare let go, his Hawken and one of the harpoons and the net slid over the edge. Impulsively, he almost lunged for the rifle, but if he did, he would follow it in.

Only then did Shakespeare remember he was not much of a swimmer. He *could*, when he had to, or occasionally for the fun of it, but he was not a seal like Zach, or even as good as Blue Water Woman. Were he to be tossed into the drink, he might never come up.

The dugout dipped into a trough between waves, giving Shakespeare a momentary respite. Then the next wave seized it and swept it aloft. Once again he braced himself, but this time, with the canoe tipped on the crest, his hand slipped. He felt himself start to fall. Only by exerting his aged sinews to their utmost was he able to avoid disaster.

The rain, the lightning, the thunder, the waves assaulted Shakespeare's senses. He lost all awareness of time, of his own self, of everything except the din and the upheaval and the rolling motion that tossed his stomach as it did the waves. He was close to being sick.

A monster wave flung the canoe toward the black clouds, and it began to roll. Shakespeare closed his eyes and fought down bitter bile. He prayed as he had not prayed in years, prayed with every fiber of his being that he would live to see Blue Water Woman again. Her face floated at the back of his eyelids. She was smiling, and she was beautiful, and he had never loved her so much as he did at that moment.

Then Shakespeare was tumbling and clawing for a hold that was not there. The shock of hitting the cold water snapped his eyes open. It snapped his mouth open, too, allowing water to gush down his throat. He swallowed and sucked in a desperate breath, but instead of air he sucked in more water.

There was a tremendous splash next to him and a glancing blow to his shoulder. Shakespeare needed to reach the surface, but he could not tell up from down or down from up. Weakly, he stroked, and went nowhere. He fought to stay conscious, but there were limits to how much punishment the human body could endure, and he had exceeded his, and then some.

Shakespeare envisioned Blue Water Woman. He wanted his last thought to be of her. He wanted to say he was sorry, and to thank her for putting up with him all these years.

Then there was nothing, nothing at all.

"You are not going out after him and that is final," Nate King said, standing in front of the cabin door, arms folded across his broad chest.

"How can you do this?" Blue Water Woman asked, tears brimming in her eyes. She had hurred to the King cabin when she discovered Shakespeare was gone. "You are his best friend."

Nate glanced at Winona, who was pouring steaming cups of tea. She sadly shook her head. "Listen to it out there," he said. Thunder conveniently boomed, stressing his point. "Look out the window." He had done so just a moment ago. "See how bad that storm is."

"All the more reason I must try to find him," Blue Water Woman pleaded. She had wanted to go out earlier, but Nate had advised her to wait until the fog broke. Now the storm had swept in, and she was so worried, her insides were twisted into a knot.

Nate gently placed his hands on her shoulders. "A canoe would not last five minutes in this storm. It would be torn to pieces." He was sorry he said it the instant the words were out of his mouth. Tears trickled down her cheeks.

"Shakespeare is in a canoe."

"Yes," Nate said, mad at his stupidity. "But he took the dugout, not the bark canoes. It will not fall apart on him."

Blue Water Woman bowed her head and her shoulders drooped. "What was he thinking?" she asked softly. "Why did he go out again? Alone?" She was hurt that he had not taken her. Even more hurt that he had not told her he was going.

Nate shrugged. "You know how he is. When he wants to do something, he never lets anything stand in his way. I am the same way."

"I warned him the water devil is bad medicine, but he would not listen," Blue Water Woman said.

"Men," Nate said. "We are all born with rocks between our ears." He grinned, but she did not grin back.

Winona came over and clasped Blue Water Woman's hand in hers. She was worried, too, greatly worried, but for her friend's sake she hid it. "Come. The tea is ready. Have a seat and calm your nerves."

"If he dies I will not want to go on living."

Winona and Nate exchanged glances, and Nate took Blue Water Woman's other hand.

"Enough of talk like that. Shakespeare is not called

Carcajou for nothing. Wolverines are the toughest animal around."

Blue Water Woman let them lead her to a chair. She slumped into it, feeling as if all the life had been drained from her body. "He is not a young man anymore. He pretends he is by ignoring his wrinkles."

Just then Evelyn came out of her bedroom. She had been listening and wished there was something she could say or do to cheer Blue Water Woman up. A bolt of lightning lit the window, and she nearly jumped. She never had liked lightning. As a little girl, during thunderstorms she would often cower in her bed with the covers over her head. "Is there anything I can do, Ma?"

Winona frowned. "There is nothing any of us can do until this storm lets up."

"I hope it stops soon."

So did Nate, but from the sound of things, it would be a while, and every moment Shakespeare spent out on the lake increased the likelihood they might never see him again.

"I am glad Dega is not out there," Evelyn said without thinking. She had him on her mind a lot of late.

"Why don't you make us some toast?" Winona suggested, distressed at her daughter's lapse.

"Sure, Ma."

Nate was glad no one else had gone with Shakespeare, or whoever did would be in the same dire straits. A thought startled him. What if someone had? He would not put it past his son to tag along, and he had not seen hide nor hair of Zach since the day before. He'd assumed Zach was tending to Louisa, but he never knew with that boy of his. "As soon as the storm ends, I am going out."

"*We* are," Blue Water Woman amended.

"He is my friend."

"He is my husband."

"The three of us will go," Winona interjected.

"I would rather you stayed here," Nate said casually, so she would not construe it as a command and be insulted.

"Three sets of eyes and ears are better than two," Winona said, as if that settled the matter.

"Four sets are better yet," Evelyn piped up.

Nate thought fast. "If all of us are out on the water, who will search the shoreline?" He left unsaid the reason: that McNair, or McNair's body, might wash up on shore. Pointing at Evelyn, he said, "I want you to ride to the Nansusequa and ask them to help you search the east shore." She would be glad to be with Dega, and she would be off the lake.

"If you want, Pa."

Nate turned to his wife. "I would like you to check in on Zach and Lou and make sure she is all right, then search along the north shore."

"I suppose I should see if Louisa has recovered," Winona reluctantly conceded.

"Blue Water Woman will search the south shore while I go out in a canoe," Nate concluded. "That way we cover all there is to cover." It made sense to him, but would it make sense to Blue Water Woman? Females had an exasperating habit of thinking they knew better than males just because they were females.

"If there is no one else to do it, very well. But if I find no trace of him, I am coming right out in a canoe."

"We will go out together," Winona told her.

Nate smothered a grin. "Whatever you two think is best."

Thunder chose that moment to rattle the dishes in the cupboard. They all gazed at the rain-lashed window.

"Oh, Carcajou." Blue Water Woman gripped the edge of the table until her knuckles were nearly white.

"He will be all right," Nate said, reading her expression.

"His heart is my heart. My heart is his." Blue Water Woman bit her lower lip.

Evelyn felt sorry for her. For some reason, the comment brought Dega to mind. "When I get married, I hope the man I care for cares for me as much as you and Shakespeare care for each other."

Winona hid her considerable surprise. That was the first time their daughter had ever mentioned marriage in a serious tone. And Evelyn had said 'when,' not 'if.'

Nate was listening to the bedlam outdoors. The storm showed no sign of abating any time soon.

"I hope you find a man like mine," Blue Water Woman said. She was sorry that she was upsetting them so much, and in an effort to cheer them, and herself, she said, "I should do as Shakespeare always says to do and look at the bright side."

"There is one?" Evelyn asked.

"All that lightning," Blue Water Woman said. "If I am lucky, it will strike that stupid steeple."

Water Womb

Warmth revived him. Blessed, wonderful warmth on his face and neck showed he was still alive.

Shakespeare McNair opened his eyes and squinted against the harsh glare of the midday sun. His face was warm, but the rest of him was cold and wet and a patchwork of pain. Blinking in the bright sunlight, he raised his head and looked about him.

The storm had ended. Far to the east a few thunderheads were visible, but otherwise the vault of sky was a pristine blue. So, too, the lake. The waves had stilled and the surface was undisturbed save for cavorting waterfowl.

"Thank God," Shakespeare croaked, his throat raw, his voice not sounding at all like it should.

The next fact he established was that he was somewhere in the middle of the lake. That he had survived at all was in no small measure due to a fluke of circumstance some might call a miracle.

The dugout was floating upside down in the water. His head, right shoulder, and right arm lay across one end. Were it not for being buoyed by the canoe, he would surely have drowned.

But how had it happened? Shakespeare wondered. The last thing he remembered was being pitched into the water. He remembered, too, hearing a loud splash that must have been the canoe crashing down next to him. The only explanation he could think of was that the canoe had gone under and bobbed back up—directly under him.

"I'll be switched," Shakespeare said, amazed at his deliverance. He patted the bottom of the dugout. Here he had poked fun at it for being a turtle in the water, and the turtle had saved his life.

But his ordeal was far from over. He had lost both paddles. He had lost his knife and his rifle and the harpoons and the net. Worse, he had lost the parfleche with his food. The lantern, too, and they only had the one. Blue Water Woman would take him to task for his carelessness.

He was alive, though, and that was the important thing. Smiling, he sat up, pleased to find he had feeling again in his left forearm. His wrist hurt where the rope had dug into his skin, but his fingers wriggled as they should. Both pistols were still tucked tight under his belt, but the soaking had rendered them useless. His ammunition pouch, powder-horn, and possibles bag had likewise been under water.

Shakespeare sought some sign of land. All he saw was water and more water. Overhead, a gull screeched. Glancing up, he said in jest, "Fetch help, will you?"

Something brushed his left foot.

Shakespeare peered into the water, but it was like peering into a mirror. He saw his reflection, not whatever had brushed against him. He moved his legs back and forth, but it was gone.

A fish, Shakespeare thought. A *small* fish. Nothing for him to worry about. His first priority was to right the dugout. To that end, he slid off and tread water and put his hands under the canoe. He figured it would be easy to flip over, but when he tried he could only lift it half a foot or so. It was just too heavy. On land he might be able to, but not in the water.

Shakespeare sighed. Here he'd thought his luck had turned. He slid his arms farther under the canoe and bunched his shoulder muscles for all he was worth, but all he did was set his gash to throbbing.

Shivering from the cold, Shakespeare reached up to pull himself out of the water. But the smooth hull defied his grasp. The Nansusequa had stripped the bark, and the hull was as smooth as glass. He had nothing to hold on to.

"When it rains, it pours," Shakespeare muttered. He had to get out of the water. The longer he was in it, the colder he would become. He might become so cold he could barely move, and once that happened, it was a slow sink to the bottom, and oblivion.

"If I ever go out on this lake again, someone should shoot me," Shakespeare said to the canoe. He refused to give up. Moving to the near end, he extended both arms and tried to wriggle and shimmy his way higher. His soaked buckskins were so slick that twice he slipped back, but at length he had half his body on the dugout. All it would take was for him to swing a leg up.

Then something brushed against his foot. Again.

Shakespeare glanced down. There could be no mistake. It was not his imagination. "Surely not," he said.

As if in answer, ten yards away a swell rose. A small one, but since the wind had died, it could only be caused by one thing.

Shakespeare scrambled higher and slipped back. He tried again and again, and each time it was the same. The whole time, the swell circled the canoe, coming closer with each pass. It was within six feet when desperation lent him extra strength. He got a leg up out of the water. That was all the extra leverage he needed.

Prone on the overturned dugout, Shakespeare watched the swell go around and around. "What are you up to, devil fish?" To reach him it would have to show itself; he half hoped it would. One look. One good look was all he wanted.

The hiss of the swell again reminded Shakespeare of the hiss of a snake. He considered using a flintlock, but his pistols were so waterlogged they would surely misfire. He turned his head in time to see the swell slow and fade as its source sank. But the fish did not dive. It hovered just below the surface. Shakespeare had the impression it was studying him even as he was trying to study it. He prodded his memory, but he had never heard of a fish that behaved like this one. None in his personal experience, either, unless he counted the time a bass paced the bull boat he was in.

"What do you want, damn you?" Shakespeare asked the great shadowy bulk. His life, most likely. But the fish would have to work for it. He was too fond of living to give up without a struggle.

Shakespeare rested his cheek on his hand. The fish could float there all day. He needed to get to land and out of his wet buckskins. "Come closer so I can shoot you."

As if it had heard, the fish swam nearer.

Shakespeare strained his eyes trying to make out details. The thing was so close he could almost reach down and touch it, and all he saw was shadow. Impulsively, he flung out a hand, and the shadow moved back out of reach.

"You are toying with me, damn you."

Suddenly the shadow erupted into motion, making another circuit of the canoe.

Taking a gamble, Shakespeare slid further down and clutched at the swell. He could not quite reach it.

Determined not to be thwarted, Shakespeare eased lower still and held his arm a few inches above the surface. The swell reappeared, sweeping around the other end of the canoe, and he smiled. He had outfoxed the finny so-and-so. Spreading his fingers, he thrust them at the onrushing water. In a twinkling his hand was immersed and he flailed about for a solid body, but all he felt was water. "Impossible!" he bellowed.

Not if the fish had dived just as he reached for it. Shakespeare had forgotten how ungodly quick the thing was. Despite its size, it was aquatic quicksilver.

The surface was once again smooth and serene.

Shakespeare clambered back up. He was tired of the cat and mouse. Most especially, he was tired of being the mouse. It was high time he used the one advantage he had over the fish: his mind. Used it right, since so far the fish had gotten the better of him at every turn. "No more," he vowed.

Shakespeare drew one of his flintlocks, thumbed back the hammer, and squeezed the trigger. As he expected, there was a *click* and nothing more. A misfire, thanks to the soaking he'd taken.

One eye on the lake, Shakespeare cleaned the weapon as best he was able, given that he did not have a dry cloth to work with. He used his sleeve to wipe the pan clean of the wet powder, then puffed to dry it, and blew down the barrel a number of times.

Opening his powder horn, Shakespeare carefully upended it over his palm. Powder trickled out.

Some was wet and some was not. He cast it over the side. He poured another handful and cast that over the side. A third handful had enough dry grains to suit him.

Shakespeare reloaded. Sliding the ramrod from its housing, he tamped a ball down the barrel. Since all his patches were soaked, he did without. The pistol should fire. He just needed to wait until the fish was right on top of him.

Waiting. That was the key. Shakespeare scanned the surface in all directions, fervently hoping the fish would come back. The minutes dragged, and he was about convinced it wouldn't, when forty yards out the swell reappeared, rising until it was a foot high. As before, the fish circled the dugout.

Shakespeare extended the flintlock but he did not shoot. *Wait*, he told himself. *Wait, wait, wait.* As the fish had done the last time, the circles were narrowing. From forty yards to thirty-five and from thirty-five to thirty. At twenty yards Shakespeare fidgeted with excitement. At ten yards his palms were sweating.

Keep coming! Shakespeare mentally shouted. Another circle or two and it would be close enough. He thumbed back the hammer.

The next time the fish swept past, it was only five yards out.

Shakespeare intended to shoot it in the head. The only other way was the heart, and he could not be sure of hitting it. As huge as the creature was, the ball might not even penetrate far enough to reach it.

Another circle, and now the fish was only four yards from Shakespeare when the swell hissed by.

Shakespeare did not move. He remembered the

time he squatted motionless for over two hours when he was after a bighorn. Compared to that, this was nothing. He sighted down the barrel and grinned when the swell filled his vision.

Only three yards out.

Then two.

Shakespeare licked his lips, but he had no spit to wet them with. His mouth was dry. He held the flintlock with both hands to steady it.

Only a yard separated the dugout from the swell as the fish coursed by for what would be the next to last time.

Shakespeare leaned down so the flintlock was practically touching the water. He shifted, eyes glued to the end of the canoe where the fish would reappear. Inwardly, he ticked off the seconds: *one, two, three, four, five*. The swell swept into sight and hissed toward him. This time the fish was practically rubbing the canoe.

Shakespeare had it dead to rights. His elbows locked, he held his breath and lightly curled his finger around the trigger. He was primed to fire.

Then the unexpected happened.

The swell slowed and split down the middle as a pea pod might split, revealing peas of a different sort: the creature's eyes. Its head rose into plain sight, and those eyes, a pair of golden peas with black in their centers, gazed up at Shakespeare. Their eyes met.

Shakespeare gasped. His whole body trembled.

The fish had stopped and was floating there, staring. It made no attempt to attack.

"No!" Shakespeare said softly.

With an almost casual sweep of its powerful tail, the fish dived.

Shakespeare stared at the bubbles that marked its

descent. He lowered the pistol and slowly let down the hammer.

Confused, doubting he had seen what he thought he saw, Shakespeare bowed his head. He sat perfectly still for the longest while. Finally, seemingly apropos of nothing, he remarked out loud, "As God is my witness, I would never have guessed."

The lake was still, the waterfowl momentarily silent. Shakespeare surveyed the blue expanse and shuddered. But not because he was still damp and the breeze was brisk. He said, "What do I do now?"

He held up the pistol and laughed. Wedging it under his belt, he swiveled onto his belly and slowly dipped his feet and legs into the water until he was half in and half out. Reaching down to grip the sides, he began kicking.

The dugout moved at a crawl, but it moved. Shakespeare reckoned it would take him the rest of the day and the better part of the night to reach land, but by God, reach it he would.

Shakespeare chuckled. A great weight had been taken off his shoulders. He sought a suitable quote to mark the occasion, but for the first time in a coon's age, he could not come up with one.

Several teal swam near and Shakespeare smiled and waved to them. "Wonderful," he muttered as he lowered his hand. "I am behaving like a perfect idiot."

His cold leg muscles were protesting and his hips were hurting, but Shakespeare ignored the pain and went on kicking. He wanted solid ground under him, wanted it more than he had just about ever wanted anything. He promised himself that if he made it back, he would fight shy of canoes for the rest of his born days. He thought of what he had almost done, and unbidden, a quote tripped from his tongue: "O monstrous arrogance. Thou liest, thou thread, thou thimble, thou yard, three-quarters, half-yard, quarter, nail, thou flea, thou nit, thou winter-cricket thou!"

He was not talking about the fish.

He was talking about himself.

A sustained hiss drew Shakespeare's attention to the return of the swell some sixty feet out.

"You again! I have made my peace! Leave me be! Don't remind an old man of his folly."

But the swell grew. It started to circle and then swung slowly toward the dugout.

"What the devil!" Shakespeare hollered. "Go eat a duck, damn you!" Expecting the swell to swerve, he made no attempt to push clear.

But the swell didn't swerve. It bore down on the canoe, rapidly gaining speed.

Appalled by the enormity of his mistake, Shakespeare shook a fist in the air. "Don't you dare! Do you hear me? Don't you dare!"

The swell kept on coming.

Aquatic Cavalry

The canoes were gone.

Nate King stood at the spot they should be, consternation flooding through him. Any hope he had of finding Shakespeare quickly had been shredded. The hurricane-force winds had sent the canoes out onto the lake, where the waves had carried them off or sunk them. But the storm was not entirely to blame. Part of the fault was his. He should have come back when the storm first hit and dragged them higher.

Hoping against hope, Nate scoured the lake, but all he saw were geese and ducks and gulls.

Nate had to get out there. He racked his brain for an idea. Building a new canoe would take too long. But there was something else he could build, something that would only take a couple of hours. With a little luck, he could complete it before the women returned and demanded to go with him.

Turning, Nate raced for his cabin. He saddled his bay and led it from the corral. Then he collected his axe and all the rope he had, climbed on, and galloped toward the woods. He knew right where to find a stand of slim pines ideal for his purpose.

Bigger trees would provide bigger logs and be safer, but felling and trimming them would take most of the day.

Rolling up his sleeves, Nate gripped the heavy axe and went to work. He swung with steady, practiced strokes, the axe biting deep. After each tree toppled, he removed the branches and shoots. He worked as fast as he could, but worry made his frantic pace seem much too slow.

Four trees were down and Nate was chopping a fifth when a feeling came over him that he was being watched. He had learned the hard way never to ignore his intuition, and he glanced up, reckoning a deer or an elk or some other animal had strayed by. But the watcher was two-legged. "You!"

"I'm happy to see you, too, Pa," Zach said dryly. He gestured at the downed saplings. "Why do you need firewood at this time of year?"

Instead of answering Nate asked, "What are you doing here? What about Lou? Should you have left her alone?"

"She practically threw me out of our cabin," Zach reported. "She was fine this morning when we woke up except for feeling a bit queasy. She sent me over to get some of those sage leaves Ma keeps on hand."

The Shoshones chewed the leaves for stomach upsets. Nate had used them on occasion himself. "I am not chopping firewood. I'm making a raft, and I could use your help."

"A raft?" Zach repeated.

Nate explained about Shakespeare taking the dugout and going back out on the lake by his lonesome. "We fear he was caught in the storm," he concluded.

"I saw some of it out my window—" Zach said, and stopped. "Dear God, Pa. Some of those waves had to be three feet high. No one could survive."

"We don't know that," Nate said angrily, and swung again, sending slivers flying. "Start hauling these to the lake. With your help I can get done in half the time."

"Sure thing. Lou will understand. She cares about that old grump as much as we do."

Nate doubted anyone other than Blue Water Woman was as fond of McNair as he was. He owed Shakespeare more than any man could ever repay. When he first came to the Rockies, he was as green as grass and would not have lived through his first winter if not for McNair's sage advice and kind help. Their bond of friendship had grown to where Nate regarded Shakespeare as more of father than a friend. His real father had always been cold and aloof, completely unlike Shakespeare. Nate sometimes wished his father had been more like his mentor, but then Nate might never have left New York for the wilds of the frontier. He would never have met Winona, never had Evelyn and Zach.

Nate was glad he had come West. He had seen things few men ever saw, lived as few men ever lived. He would not trade his experiences for all the jade in China. Yes, life in the wilderness was fraught with danger, but every pearl, it was said, came at great price, and the pearl of true freedom, of being able to live as he wanted without let or hindrance, was worth the perils that had to be overcome.

"Pa?"

Nate realized his son was trying to get his attention. He looked up. "What is it?"

"You can stop chopping," Zach said, and pointed.

Blue Water Woman was riding along the water's edge toward Nate's cabin. She had a rope in one hand. The other end was tied to a bark canoe she was pulling after her.

"Let's go," Nate said. Hastening to the bay, he climbed on and galloped to meet her. She spotted them, and was off her horse and untying the rope from the canoe when they reined to a stop.

"Where did you find it?" Nate asked as he alighted.

"Washed up on the shore." Blue Water Woman glanced at where the canoes had been before the storm struck. "There wasn't one for you to use? It is a good thing I brought it, then."

"I was making a raft," Nate explained. He looked in the canoe; the paddles were missing. He mentioned the loss, adding, "I have one at my place. But only one," he emphasized.

Blue Water Woman patted the canoe. "Finding this is an omen. I am going with you, and I will not brook no for an answer." Something more than simple anxiety was telling her she must hasten out on the lake after her man.

"What about me?" Zach asked.

"You were fetching sage for Louisa, remember?" Nate reminded him. He was unhappy with Blue Water Woman's decision, but he had no right to stop her.

"She won't mind if I help out."

"Three in the canoe would be too crowded."

Blue Water Woman looked at Nate and impatiently motioned to the water. "Why are we still standing here? Hurry and fetch that paddle."

The breeze was at their backs when they pushed off. Nate knelt in the bow; Blue Water Woman was in the stern, her hands clasped in her lap. To look at her, at how calm she was, no one would guess what she must have been going through.

"You are holding up better than I am," Nate commented, as he dipped the paddle in the water and stroked.

"Have you ever been attacked by a mountain lion?" Blue Water Woman asked.

Nate recalled a harrowing encounter he'd had with one of the big cats years ago. "Yes. Why?"

"There is a mountain lion loose inside me. It is ripping my stomach and clawing my heart, and if we do not find my Carcajou, it will tear me apart."

The lake spread out in a blue-green sheen before them. Here and there were ducks, singly and in pairs and squadrons. Geese honked and plunged their long necks into the lake after fish. Gulls wheeled white in the sky, their high-pitched cries letting the world know they were there.

Blue Water Woman shielded her eyes from the glare and peered all about. "Where *is* he?"

"We will find him," Nate said, more to boost her spirits than out of an unshakable conviction that they would.

"Were it not for his white hairs, I would do as white women do with their young and put him over my knee and spank him."

"Spank him anyway," Nate said. "It would serve him right."

Blue Water Woman mustered a grin to be polite. "I have never understood that."

"What?" Nate said, preoccupied with ripples to the northeast he could not account for.

"Hitting a child. My people think it is bad medicine. So do the Shoshones."

"I know," Nate said. Shortly after Winona had announced she was pregnant for the first time, they sat down and talked about how they wished they could tell whether the baby was a boy or a girl, and what names they liked, and how they would go about rearing it, no matter which it was. At one point he had joked, "If we have a daughter, you will have to do the spanking. I could spank a boy, but never a girl."

Winona had asked him what spanking was, and when he explained, she had recoiled in horror, then went on to say that for a Shoshone, the idea was unthinkable. "Hit a child and you wound their heart for life."

"I turned out all right," Nate told her. "And my father tarred the dickens out of me at least once a week."

Appalled, Winona insisted there would be no tarring in the King family. Nate, as he always did, respected her wishes. But there had been times—

"Nate?" Blue Water Woman said. "Do you see them, too?"

Nate nodded. She was referring to the ripples he had noticed. They had grown in number and size. Something under the surface was agitating the water. Something big, by the looks of it.

"Could it be the water devil?"

Nate had been wondering the same thing. He steered the canoe toward them and almost immediately the ripples vanished.

Blue Water Woman sat forward and declared, "It *is* the water devil!"

Nate was not so sure. It could be anything. Plenty of big, ordinary fish inhabited the lake. He came to the approximate spot and leaned over to probe the depths, but it was like trying to see the bottom of a well.

Blue Water Woman was bent over the other side. "Do you see anything? Anything at all?"

"No." Nate resumed stroking. The splash of his paddle and the honking of nearby geese nearly drowned out a loud splash. He looked but saw only ripples.

"What was that?"

"A fish," Nate said. "The kind we like to fry in a pan."

"I thought I saw a fin," Blue Water Woman said. "A huge fin," she emphasized. "It must be the water devil. It has killed my husband, and now it is after us."

"You are jumping to conclusions," Nate warned. Which for her was unusual. Out of all of them, she had always been the most level-headed. Even more so than his wife.

"It will return," Blue Water Woman predicted. "When it does, you will see for yourself." She put a hand on the pistol at her waist. "For what it has done to my husband, it deserves to die."

"There you go again," Nate said. "Sit back, will you?" Her weight was not enough to tip the canoe, but she was leaning much too far out.

"There!" Blue Water Woman exclaimed, jabbing a finger. "I told you!"

All Nate saw were a few small ripples. "That could be a minnow," he teased her.

"I saw the head. It was peeking at us."

"Peeking?" Nate repeated, and chuckled.

"That is not the right word?" Blue Water Woman took pride in her mastery of the white tongue. She was not as adept as Winona, but she flattered herself that she spoke it fluently.

Nate went on chuckling. "It fits, I suppose." But the notion was as silly as a grizzly bear peeking from behind a tree. "Whatever it is, it's not bother-ing us." He rose higher to search directly ahead. "We shouldn't forget why we are out here."

"As if I ever could," Blue Water Woman said somberly. Long ago she had accepted that one day she might lose her husband. He was older, and he insisted on taking risks men his age should not take. But she had never imagined it would end like *this*. As she had been doing all morning, she reached out with her heart, seeking some sign that he was still alive. Often when he was away from her, she could feel him deep inside, but now she felt only a strange coldness. That, more than anything else, scared her, scared her terribly.

"When we find him we will have a good laugh over all of this," Nate remarked.

"Have you been drinking?"

Nate snorted. He was not much for hard liquor. Every now and again he treated himself to a little brandy, usually on a winter's eve in front of the fire-place, but that was the extent of it. "I rarely do and you—"

The canoe gave an abrupt lurch, as if they had collided with a submerged object. Instantly, Nate dipped the paddle in to bring them to a stop, then checked on both sides. "What was that?"

"The water devil." Blue Water Woman did not look. She drew her pistol and held it in her lap.

Nate continued paddling. They went ten feet with-out incident—twenty feet—thirty. Some of the ten-sion started to drain from him. Suddenly the canoe gave another lurch. He started to bend over the gun-wale. There was a loud *bump* from below, and the ca-noe rose out of the water a few inches and settled back again.

"Do you believe me now, Horatio?"

Under less harrowing circumstances Nate would have laughed. She never call him that. Only Shakespeare did. "I believe you."

Ripples appeared in front of them and moved slowly off to the east.

"Follow it," Blue Water Woman directed.

"But Shakespeare—"

"If he were alive, I would know." Blue Water Woman raised her pistol. "Understand this. I intend to kill it. You can help, or I will come back out by myself. Either way, it is going to die."

Nate did not reply. But she was not thinking straight. Her pistol would have no more effect than a pebble. He stroked harder, regretting that they did not have a harpoon.

"Faster," Blue Water Woman urged. "Bring us up next to it."

"What good will that do?" Nate asked. But he did as she wanted. The ripples were moving so slowly that he easily caught up and paced them. "Now what?" he asked, glancing over his shoulder. He thought she would take a shot. But she had something else in mind.

Blue Water Woman set her pistol down and drew her knife. In a swift, fluid movement, she stood, whipped her dress off over her head, dropped it at her feet, and dived over the side.

The Heart of Darkness

Blue Water Woman was a Salish. The whites called them Flatheads. The whites also called the lake at the heart of Salish territory Flathead Lake. To her, growing up, the lake had been as much a part of her life as the grass and the trees and the sky. She could swim by the time she had seen six winters. Thereafter, she spent every free minute she could in or near the water. Her fondness went far beyond that of any other Salish. So much so, that she earned the name Blue Water Woman.

Now she lived up to that name. She cleaved the water with barely a splash and swam with the agility of a seal. Ahead loomed a dark mass. She had been right. It *was* the water devil, and it was swimming slowly along, as if water devils did not have a care in the world.

Her mouth clamped tight and her lungs filled with air, Blue Water Woman pumped her arms and legs. It did not turn or look back. Either it was unaware she had dived in or it did not regard her as a threat.

Blue Water Woman clutched her knife more firmly. She thought of Shakespeare, the man who meant more to her than the breath she was holding, who meant more to her than anything, and her resolve to kill the beast became an iron rod of vengeance.

She did not care how big the thing was. She did not care that it could kill her with a casual swat of its huge tail. She did not care about anything except avenging the other half of her heart.

She gained quickly, swimming wide of the tail and then angling toward the great bulk of the body. Inwardly she smiled at the image of plunging her blade in again and again. She was almost close enough, the thing was almost within reach of her knife, when something seized hold of her ankle.

Nate King could not say which had shocked him more: that Blue Water Woman had stripped naked right there in front of him, or that she had thrown herself into the water after the water devil. But he had not lived as long as he had in the wilds by letting shock slow his reflexes. No sooner had the water swallowed her than he was up and stripping off his pistols and possibles bag and powder horn and ammunition pouch. Then he dived in after her.

Nate spotted her right away, swimming with amazing swiftness. He swam after her and discovered that while he had always been accounted a powerful swimmer, she was faster. He was a catfish, she was a bass. He tried to catch her and couldn't. The realization that if he didn't, she might die, lent extra energy to his limbs, but she still stayed ahead of him.

The fish filled his vision. This close, there could be no doubt what it was. An enormous fish, the most enormous he'd ever seen, the most enormous he'd ever heard off. No doubt there were bigger fish in the oceans and elsewhere. But in *this* lake at *this* moment, *this* fish was a leviathan.

The thing could slay either of them as easily as they could slay a tiny guppy.

Fear for Blue Water Woman spurred Nate into exerting his all. She swam wide to avoid the tail, and in doing so, enabled him to narrow the gap, enough that by hurtling forward, he was able to grab her right ankle and hold fast.

Blue Water Woman glanced back. The fire of her vengeance became the fire of resentment. She jerked her leg, but Nate would not let go. Twisting, she pushed his arm, but could not move it. She glared at him and saw he was not looking at her but at something behind her. She sensed movement and knew what she would see before she turned.

The fish seemed to fill the lake. It floated an arm's length away, staring at her, its head in shadow. By some trick of the light she could see its eyes. They gleamed like twin embers, but not with fury, or with hate, or with any emotion as humans understood them. Blue Water Woman looked into those eyes and the emotion she saw, if a fish could be said to have emotion, was sadness, a deep, pervading sorrow such as she had seldom beheld in any person or animal. It stunned her. She did not move as the fish came closer, until it was so near they were practically touching.

Blue Water Woman looked, and she could not stab it. She looked into those eyes and she would never be the same again.

Then it was gone. A flick of its tail and fish dived for the dark depths it called home.

Blue Water Woman shook herself to break the spell. She felt Nate tug on her ankle. He gestured toward the surface and she nodded. Together, they swam up and gulped air.

"Are you all right?" Nate asked.

"I am fine," Blue Water Woman lied.

Nate swam to their canoe, climbed in, and offered her his hand. "Let me help you up."

Blue Water Woman started toward him.

"Out for some exercise, are you?"

They turned. Coming toward them, on his knees in the bow of the dugout and paddling with his hands, was a white-haired devil of a different sort, wearing a grin a mile wide.

"Shakespeare!" Nate exploded. "We found you!"

"I would argue that I found you, Horatio, since I saw you first."

Blue Water Woman squealed in delight and stroked to the dugout. "Carcajou!" she cried. "You are alive!" Pulling herself up, she threw herself into his open arms and clung to him as if to life itself.

"You are getting me wet, woman," Shakespeare grumbled. "And I was just starting to dry out."

"I have been in the water," Blue Water Woman said huskily, her face pressed to his neck.

"In the middle of the lake?"

"I thought you were dead. I was avenging you."

Shakespeare looked down at her. "Do you always do your avenging in the altogether?"

"You noticed."

"Men always notice little things like naked women. All a woman has to do is take off her clothes, and she is a regular sensation."

"I have missed you." Blue Water Woman kissed him and closed her misting eyes.

"Not so fast, wench. Here I am gone for a while, and I come back to find you cavorting with my best friend."

"Behave. He saved me from making a mistake."

"He was a mite slow," Shakespeare said.

"Not that," Blue Water Woman responded in mild exasperation. "I was going to stab the water devil."

Shakespeare gripped her shoulders and pushed her back. "You didn't! God in heaven, tell me you didn't."

"I didn't."

Shakespeare exhaled in relief.

Nate was not following any of this. "Hold on. You were the one who kept saying the thing was a menace and had to be killed. I thought that was what all this was about?"

"Since when do you listen to me?" Shakespeare rejoined.

"I am serious. We have gone to all this bother. The steeple. The canoes. Lou nearly drowing. And now you are saying it was all for nothing? That you have changed your mind and don't want the thing dead?"

"That is pretty much it, yes. Remember the Bard. He said that the quality of mercy is not strained; it droppeth as the gentle rain from heaven."

Nate shook his head in bewilderment. "You are as fickle as the weather. Next you will be saying that it was a mistake for us to come out after it."

"A mistake and then some," Shakespeare concurred. "What merit were it in death to take this poor maid from the world?"

"Are we talking about a woman or the creature?

"Ah, Horatio!" Shakespeare beamed. "A fellow of infinite jest, of most excellent fancy."

"I can never tell when you are serious."

"I am always serious," Shakespeare said. "Except when I'm not."

"You are a lunatic."

"And you have not so much brain as ear wax."

"Enough." Blue Water Woman pecked her husband on the chin. "Stop teasing him, Carcajou. Why have you changed your mind about the water devil?"

"Fish," Shakespeare said. "It is a *fish*. Not a water devil. Nor a beast. Not a monster or a demon or a creature. It is a plain and simple fish."

"I have looked into its eyes," Blue Water Woman said, and shuddered.

"*Et tu?*" Shakespeare quoted. "And what did you see in them? What did your womanly intuition tell you?"

Blue Water Woman hesitated. "I am not certain."

"I am," Shakespeare said. "Have I mentioned that it saved me? That the dugout had capsized and I could not right it? And the fish did it for me?"

Nate started to laugh but caught himself. "Wait. The fish has gone from menace to savior? I take my words back. You are not as fickle as the weather. You are *more* fickle than the weather."

"The answer is there, Horatio, if you but have the eyes to see," Shakespeare said.

"I don't even know the question."

Shakespeare swept an arm at the watery expanse in which their canoes were drifting. "My mistake was one anyone could make. After those incidents we had, I jumped to the conclusion the fish was out to harm us. To be honest, I didn't think it *was* a fish. I figured it was a holdout from the dawn of time, and that when we cornered it, it would turn out to be something completely new. Or, I should say, completely old."

"I never saw a fish like this one," Nate said.

"It is unique. But it wasn't always. It had to come

from somewhere, and that somewhere was other fish."

"You are taking the long way around the bush."

"Straight tongue, then," Shakespeare said. "The fish was not trying to harm us. It wanted to be friends."

Nate had heard his mentor express some peculiar notions over the years, but this one beat them all, and he declared as much.

Shakespeare sighed. "Pay attention. I am the schoolmarm and you are the student." He dipped his hand into the lake and held it out as the drops splattered the surface. "This lake is your home. Once—"

"Mine?" Nate interrupted. "I am a fish now?"

"If I had a tree limb I would beat you. Let me finish." Shakespeare paused. "Now, as I was saying, this lake is your home and you share it with others of your kind. But one by one they age and die until you are the last one left. The other fish in the lake are not the same. You share the lake with them, but you are as different from them as an elk is from ants. Do you savvy so far?"

"As strange as it sounds, you almost make sense."

"Good. So you are the last, and you go on living, year after year, winter after winter. But you have no one to call a companion. There is you and only you, and you are as lonesome as lonesome can be."

"Oh, brother," Nate said.

"Then one day new critters show up. Two-legged varmints who spend a lot of time near and in the water. You hear them. You smell them. Naturally, you want to find out more about them, so you swim close to them a few times, and because you do not realize how big and strong you are, you break their fishing line and knock one of them over when you push in too close to shore."

Nate's eyes widened. "You are not suggesting—"

Shakespeare did not let him finish. "I certainly am. The fish was never out to harm us. It was curious, is all. Curious and friendly, and its friendliness nearly got some of us killed."

"It is a fish," Nate said.

"Yes. We have established that fact. For a student you are an awful dunce."

"You make it sound almost human. You don't *know* it was only curious. You don't *know* it was only being friendly."

"It fetched you to me, didn't it?"

"I must have missed that part," Nate said.

"You were following it, weren't you? And it led you right to me. I think it was trying to help."

"I think I need a drink." Nate looked at Blue Water Woman, who had been strangely quiet. "What do you think?"

"I think I would like to put my dress on."

Embarrassed by his oversight, Nate scooped it up, brought his canoe over alongside the dugout, and, averting his eyes, held the dress out. "Sorry. I should have done this sooner."

Blue Water Woman went to slip it on, then glanced at Shakespeare. "You too."

"Me what?"

"Look the other way."

"This is the silliest stuff that ever I heard," Shakespeare quoted. "I am your husband. I have seen you bare more times than I have fingers and toes times a thousand."

"Nonetheless, you will look the other way. And when we get back, you will take down your steeple.

And you will never again, for as long as we live, sneak out onto this lake or any other by yourself. Agreed?"

"There's villainy abroad."

"If there is, it is yours, not mine. Are we agreed?"

"A stewed prune has more faith than you," Shakespeare resorted to the Bard. "Very well. No looking, no steeple, no sneaking. Is there anything else your humble slave might do for her majesty?"

"Get us to shore. Right away, if you please."

"I don't have a paddle."

"Then we will climb in with Nate. But we will not stay out here an instant longer than we have to."

Shakespeare sighed. "You heard the lady, Horatio. We are coming aboard."

"And that's it?" Nate said. "We let the fish live and go on with our lives as if nothing ever happened?"

"Remember what the Bard said." Shakespeare responded with a weary smile. "All's well that ends well."

Author's Note

As long-time readers of the popular *Wilderness* series are aware, Nate King, like many mountain men,
loved to tell tall tales. He relates a number of them
in his journal.

In order to truly show Nate's character and quirks,
I have taken the liberty of turning some of those tall
tales into stories. *The Lost Valley* and *Fang and Claw*
are two of the more notable. (Some would add *Mountain Devil* to the list, but I leave it up to you whether
such creatures as Sasquatch or Bigfoot exist.)

Which brings us to *In Darkest Depths*. It, too, might
qualify as a tall tale, except that in his journal Nate
states that the events really happened and were not
a figment of his brandy-influenced imagination.

As with *Mountain Devil*, you must decide whether
to believe or disbelieve. I would only note certain
news accounts, some of which you might have heard,
where incredibly huge fish have been pulled from
lakes and rivers and even ponds.

Perhaps, to take a page from McNair's passion,
there are more things in heaven and earth than are
dreamt of in our philosophy.

Enjoy the Wilderness series by
David Thompson
from the very beginning!